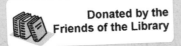
It is not that I was credulous, simply that I believed in all things dark and dangerous. It was part of my young creed that the night was full of ghosts and witches, hungry and flapping and dressed completely in black.

The converse held reassuringly true: daylight was safe. Daylight was always safe.

Other Books for Young Readers by
NEIL GAIMAN

Coraline

The Wolves in the Walls

The Day I Swapped My Dad
for Two Goldfish

MirrorMask

The Dangerous Alphabet

By Neil Gaiman and Michael Reaves
InterWorld

NEIL GAIMAN

M Is for Magic

Illustrations by
TEDDY KRISTIANSEN

HARPERTROPHY®
An Imprint of HarperCollinsPublishers

EL DORADO COUNTY LIBRARY
345 FAIR LANE
PLACERVILLE, CA 95667

M Is for Magic

Compilation copyright © 2007 by Neil Gaiman

"Introduction" © 2007 by Neil Gaiman.

"The Case of the Four and Twenty Blackbirds" © 1984 by Neil Gaiman. First published
in *Knave*.

"Troll Bridge" © 1993 by Neil Gaiman. First published in *Snow White, Blood Red*.

"Don't Ask Jack" © 1995 by Neil Gaiman. First published in Overstreet's *FAN* magazine.

"How to Sell the Ponti Bridge" © 1985 by Neil Gaiman. First published in *Imagine* #24.

"October in the Chair" © 2002 by Neil Gaiman. First published in *Conjunctions* no. 39.

"Chivalry" © 1993 by Neil Gaiman. First published in *Snow White, Blood Red*.

"The Price" © 1997 by Neil Gaiman. First published as a chapbook by DreamHaven Press.

"How to Talk to Girls at Parties" © 2006 by Neil Gaiman. First published in *Fragile Things*.

"Sunbird" © 2005 by Neil Gaiman. First published in *Noisy Outlaws, Unfriendly Blobs,
and Some Other Things That Aren't as Scary, Maybe, Depending on How You Feel About
Lost Lands, Stray Cellphones, Creatures from the Sky, Parents Who Disappear in Peru, a
Man Named Lars Farf, and One Other Story We Couldn't Quite Finish, So Maybe You
Could Help Us Out.*

"The Witch's Headstone" © 2007 by Neil Gaiman. First published in *Wizards: Magical
Tales from the Masters of Modern Fantasy*.

"Instructions" © 2000 by Neil Gaiman. First published in *A Wolf at the Door*.

Illustrations copyright © 2007 by Teddy Kristiansen

Library of Congress Cataloging-in-Publication Data is available.

ISBN 978-0-06-118647-9 (pbk.)

Typography by Hilary Zarycky

❖

First Harper Trophy edition, 2008

15 16 OPM 12 11

Writing imaginative tales for the young
is like sending coals to Newcastle. For coals.

Contents

Introduction

WHEN I WAS YOUNG, and it doesn't really seem that long ago, I loved books of short stories. Short stories could be read from start to finish in the kind of times I had available for reading—morning break, or after-lunch nap, or on trains. They'd set up, they'd roll, and they'd take you to a new world and deliver you safely back to school or back home in half an hour or so.

Stories you read when you're the right age never quite leave you. You may forget who wrote them or what the story was called. Sometimes you'll forget precisely what happened, but if a story touches you it will stay with you, haunting the places in your mind that you rarely ever visit.

Horror stays with you hardest. If it brings a real chill to the back of your neck, if once the story is done you find yourself closing the book slowly, for fear of disturbing something, and creeping away, then it's there for the rest of time. There was a story I read when I was nine that ended with a room covered with snails. I think they were probably man-eating snails, and they were crawling slowly toward someone to eat him. I get the same creeps remembering it now that I did when I read it.

Fantasy gets into your bones. There's a curve in a road I sometimes pass, a view of a village on rolling green hills, and, behind it, huger, craggier, grayer hills and, in the distance, mountains and mist, that I cannot see without remembering reading *The Lord of the Rings*. The book is somewhere inside me, and that view brings it to the surface.

And science fiction (although there's only a little of that here, I'm afraid) takes you across the stars, and into other times and minds. There's nothing like spending some time inside an alien head to remind us how little divides us, person from person.

Short stories are tiny windows into other worlds and other minds and other dreams. They are journeys you can make to the far side of the universe and still be back in time for dinner.

I've been writing short stories for almost a quarter of a century now. In the beginning they were a great way to begin to learn my craft as a writer. The hardest thing to do as a young writer is to finish something, and that was what I was learning how to do. These days most of the things I write are long—long comics or long books or long films—and a short story, something that's finished and over in a weekend or a week, is pure fun.

My favorite short story writers as a boy are, many of them, my favorite short story writers now. People like Saki or Harlan Ellison, like John Collier or Ray Bradbury. Close-up conjurors, who, with just twenty-six letters and a handful of punctuation marks, could make you laugh and break your heart, all in a handful of pages.

There's another good thing about a book of short stories: you don't have to like them all. If there's one you don't enjoy, well, there will be another one along soon.

The stories in here will take you from a hard-boiled detective story about nursery rhyme characters to a group of people who like to eat things, from a poem about how to behave if you find yourself in a fairy tale to a story about a boy who runs into a troll beneath a bridge and the bargain they make.

There's a story that will be part of my next children's book, *The Graveyard Book*, about a boy who lives in a graveyard and is brought up by dead people, and there's a story that I wrote when I was a very young writer called "How to Sell the Ponti Bridge," a fantasy story inspired by a man named "Count" Victor Lustig who really did sell the Eiffel Tower in much the same way (and who died in Alcatraz prison some years later). There are a couple of slightly scary stories, and a couple of mostly funny ones, and a bunch of them that aren't quite one thing or another, but I hope you'll like them anyway.

When I was a boy, Ray Bradbury picked stories from his books of short stories he thought younger readers might like, and he published them as *R Is for Rocket* and *S Is for Space*. Now I was doing the same sort of thing, and I asked Ray if he'd mind if I called this book *M Is for Magic*. (He didn't.)

M *is* for magic. All the letters are, if you put them together properly. You can make magic with them, and dreams, and, I hope, even a few surprises. . . .

NEIL GAIMAN
August 2006

M Is for Magic

The Case of the Four and Twenty Blackbirds

I SAT IN MY OFFICE, nursing a glass of hooch and idly cleaning my automatic. Outside the rain fell steadily, like it seems to do most of the time in our fair city, whatever the tourist board says. Heck, I didn't care. I'm not on the tourist board. I'm a private dick, and one of the best, although you wouldn't have known it; the office was crumbling, the rent was unpaid, and the hooch was my last.

Things are tough all over.

To cap it all the only client I'd had all week never showed up on the street corner where I'd waited for him. He said it was going to be a big job, but now I'd never know: he kept a prior appointment in the morgue.

So when the dame walked into my office I was sure my luck had changed for the better.

"What are you selling, lady?"

She gave me a look that would have induced

heavy breathing in a pumpkin, and which shot my heartbeat up to three figures. She had long blonde hair and a figure that would have made Thomas Aquinas forget his vows. I forgot all mine about never taking cases from dames.

"What would you say to some of the green stuff?" she asked in a husky voice, getting straight to the point.

"Continue, sister." I didn't want her to know how bad I needed the dough, so I held my hand in front of my mouth; it doesn't help if a client sees you salivate.

She opened her purse and flipped out a photograph. Glossy eight by ten. "Do you recognize that man?"

In my business you know who people are. "Yeah."

"He's dead."

"I know that too, sweetheart. It's old news. It was an accident."

Her gaze went so icy you could have chipped it into cubes and cooled a cocktail with it. "My brother's death was no accident."

I raised an eyebrow—you need a lot of arcane skills in my business—and said, "Your brother, eh?"

Funny, she hadn't struck me as the type that had brothers.

"I'm Jill Dumpty."

"So your brother was Humpty Dumpty?"

"And he didn't fall off that wall, Mr. Horner. He was pushed."

Interesting, if true. Dumpty had his finger in most of the crooked pies in town; I could think of five guys who would have preferred to see him dead than alive without trying. Without trying too hard, anyway.

"You seen the cops about this?"

"Nah. The King's Men aren't interested in anything to do with his death. They say they did all they could do in trying to put him together again after the fall."

I leaned back in my chair.

"So what's it to you. Why do you need me?"

"I want you to find the killer, Mr. Horner. I want him brought to justice. I want him to fry like an egg. Oh—and one other *little* thing," she added lightly. "Before he died Humpty had a small manila envelope full of photographs he was meant to be sending me. Medical photos. I'm a trainee nurse, and I need them to pass my finals."

I inspected my nails, then looked up at her face, taking in a handful of waist and several curves on the way up. She was a looker, although her cute nose was a little on the shiny side. "I'll take the case. Seventy-five a day and two hundred bonus for results."

She smiled; my stomach twisted around once and went into orbit. "You get another two hundred if you get me those photographs. I want to be a nurse real bad." Then she dropped three fifties on my desktop.

I let a devil-may-care grin play across my rugged face. "Say, sister, how about letting me take you out for dinner? I just came into some money."

She gave an involuntary shiver of anticipation and muttered something about having a thing about midgets, so I knew I was onto a good thing. Then she gave me a lopsided smile that would have made Albert Einstein drop a decimal point. "First find my brother's killer, Mr. Horner. And my photographs. *Then* we can play."

She closed the door behind her. Maybe it was still raining but I didn't notice. I didn't care.

*

There are parts of town the tourist board doesn't mention. Parts of town where the police travel in threes if they travel at all. In my line of work you get to visit them more than is healthy. Healthy is never.

He was waiting for me outside Luigi's. I slid up behind him, my rubber-soled shoes soundless on the shiny wet sidewalk.

"Hiya, Cock."

He jumped and spun around; I found myself gazing up into the muzzle of a .45. "Oh, Horner." He put the gun away. "Don't call me Cock. I'm Bernie Robin to you, short-stuff, and don't you forget it."

"Cock Robin is good enough for me, Cock. Who killed Humpty Dumpty?"

He was a strange-looking bird, but you can't be choosy in my profession. He was the best underworld lead I had.

"Let's see the color of your money."

I showed him a fifty.

"Hell," he muttered. "It's green. Why can't they make puce or mauve money for a change?" He took it though. "All I know is that the Fat Man had his finger in a lot of pies."

"So?"

"One of those pies had four and twenty blackbirds in it."

"Huh?"

"Do I hafta spell it out for you? I . . . ughh—" He crumpled to the sidewalk, an arrow protruding from his back. Cock Robin wasn't going to be doing any more chirping.

Sergeant O'Grady looked down at the body, then he looked down at me. "Faith and begorrah, to be sure," he said. "If it isn't Little Jack Horner himself."

"I didn't kill Cock Robin, Sarge."

"And I suppose that the call we got down at the station telling us you were going to be rubbing the late Mr. Robin out—here, tonight—was just a hoax?"

"If I'm the killer, where are my arrows?" I thumbed open a pack of gum and started to chew. "It's a frame."

He puffed on his meerschaum and then put it away, and idly played a couple of phrases of the *William Tell* overture on his oboe. "Maybe. Maybe not. But you're still a suspect. Don't leave town. And, Horner . . ."

"Yeah?"

"Dumpty's death was an accident. That's what the coroner said. That's what I say. Drop the case."

I thought about it. Then I thought of the money, and the girl. "No dice, Sarge."

He shrugged. "It's your funeral." He said it like it probably would be.

I had a funny feeling he could be right.

"You're out of your depth, Horner. You're playing with the big boys. And it ain't healthy."

From what I could remember of my school days he was correct. Whenever I played with the big boys I always wound up having the stuffing beaten out of me. But how did O'Grady—how *could* O'Grady have known that? Then I remembered something else.

O'Grady was the one that used to beat me up the most.

It was time for what we in the profession call legwork. I made a few discreet inquiries around town, but found out nothing about Dumpty that I didn't know already.

Humpty Dumpty was a bad egg. I remembered

him when he was new in town, a smart young animal trainer with a nice line in training mice to run up clocks. He went to the bad pretty fast though; gambling, drink, women, it's the same story all over. A bright young kid thinks that the streets of Nurseryland are paved with gold, and by the time he finds out otherwise it's much too late.

Dumpty started off with extortion and robbery on a small scale—he trained up a team of spiders to scare little girls away from their curds and whey, which he'd pick up and sell on the black market. Then he moved on to blackmail—the nastiest game. We crossed paths once, when I was hired by this young society kid—let's call him Georgie Porgie—to recover some compromising snaps of him kissing the girls and making them cry. I got the snaps, but I learned it wasn't healthy to mess with the Fat Man. And I don't make the same mistakes twice. Hell, in my line of work I can't afford to make the same mistakes once.

It's a tough world out there. I remember when Little Bo Peep first came to town . . . but you don't want to hear my troubles. If you're not dead yet, you've got troubles of your own.

I checked out the newspaper files on Dumpty's death. One minute he was sitting on a wall, the next he was in pieces at the bottom. All the King's Horses and all the King's Men were on the scene in minutes, but he needed more than first aid. A medic named Foster was called—a friend of Dumpty's from his Gloucester days—although I don't know of anything a doc can do when you're dead.

Hang on a second—*Dr. Foster!*

I got that old feeling you get in my line of work. Two little brain cells rub together the right way and in seconds you've got a twenty-four-karat cerebral fire on your hands.

You remember the client who didn't show—the one I'd waited for all day on the street corner? An accidental death. I hadn't bothered to check it out—I can't afford to waste time on clients who aren't going to pay for it.

Three deaths, it seemed. Not one.

I reached for the telephone and rang the police station. "This is Horner," I told the desk man. "Lemme speak to Sergeant O'Grady."

There was a crackling and he came on the line. "O'Grady speaking."

"It's Horner."

"Hi, Little Jack." That was just like O'Grady. He'd been kidding me about my size since we were kids together. "You finally figured out that Dumpty's death was accidental?"

"Nope. I'm now investigating three deaths. The Fat Man's, Bernie Robin's, and Dr. Foster's."

"Foster the plastic surgeon? His death was an accident."

"Sure. And your mother was married to your father."

There was a pause. "Horner, if you phoned me up just to talk dirty, I'm not amused."

"Okay, wise guy. If Humpty Dumpty's death was an accident and so was Dr. Foster's, tell me just one thing.

"Who killed Cock Robin?" I don't ever get accused of having too much imagination, but there's one thing I'd swear to. I could *hear* him grinning over the phone as he said: "You did, Horner. And I'm staking my badge on it."

The line went dead.

My office was cold and lonely, so I wandered down

to Joe's Bar for some companionship and a drink or three.

Four and twenty blackbirds. A dead doctor. The Fat Man. Cock Robin . . . Heck, this case had more holes in it than Swiss cheese and more loose ends than a torn string vest. And where did the juicy Miss Dumpty come into it? Jack and Jill—we'd make a great team. When this was all over perhaps we could go off together to Louie's little place on the hill, where no one's interested in whether you got a marriage license or not. The Pail of Water, that was the name of the joint.

I called the bartender over. "Hey, Joe."

"Yeah, Mr. Horner?" He was polishing a glass with a rag that had seen better days as a shirt.

"Did you ever meet the Fat Man's sister?"

He scratched at his cheek. "Can't say as I did. His sister . . . huh? Hey—the Fat Man didn't have a sister."

"You sure of that?"

"Sure I'm sure. It was the day my sister had her first kid—I told the Fat Man I was an uncle. He gave me this look and says, 'Ain't no way I'll ever be an uncle, Joe. Got no sisters or brothers, nor no other kinfolk neither.'"

If the mysterious Miss Dumpty wasn't his sister, who *was* she?

"Tell me, Joe. Didja ever see him in here with a dame—about so high, shaped like this?" My hands described a couple of parabolas. "Looks like a blonde love goddess."

He shook his head. "Never saw him with any dames. Recently he was hanging around with some medical guy, but the only thing he ever cared about was those crazy birds and animals of his."

I took a swig of my drink. It nearly took the roof of my mouth off. "Animals? I thought he'd given all that up."

"Naw—couple weeks back he was in here with a whole bunch of blackbirds he was training to sing 'Wasn't that a dainty dish to set before *mmm mmm.*'"

"*Mmm mmm?*"

"Yeah. I got no idea who."

I put my drink down. A little of it spilt on the counter, and I watched it strip the paint. "Thanks, Joe. You've been a big help." I handed him a ten-dollar bill. "For information received," I said—adding,

"Don't spend it all at once."

In my profession it's making little jokes like that that keeps you sane.

I had one contact left. Ma Hubbard. I found a pay phone and called her number.

"Old Mother Hubbard's Cupboard—Cake Shop and licensed Soup Kitchen."

"It's Horner, Ma."

"Jack? It ain't safe for me to talk to you."

"For old time's sake, sweetheart. You owe me a favor." Some two-bit crooks had once knocked off the Cupboard, leaving it bare. I'd tracked them down and returned the cakes and soup.

"Okay. But I don't like it."

"*You* know everything that goes on around here on the food front, Ma. What's the significance of a pie with four and twenty trained blackbirds in it?"

She whistled long and low. "You really don't know?"

"I wouldn't be asking you if I did."

"You should read the Court pages of the papers next time, sugar. Jeez. You are out of your depth."

"C'mon, Ma. Spill it."

"It so happens that that particular dish was set before the King a few weeks back. . . . Jack? Are you still there?"

"I'm still here, ma'am," I said quietly. "All of a sudden a lot of things are starting to make sense." I put down the phone.

It was beginning to look like Little Jack Horner had pulled out a plum from this pie.

It was raining, steady and cold. I phoned a cab.

Quarter of an hour later one lurched out of the darkness.

"You're late."

"So complain to the tourist board."

I climbed in the back, wound down the window, and lit a cigarette.

And I went to see the Queen.

The door to the private part of the palace was locked. It's the part that the public don't get to see. But I've never been public, and the little lock hardly slowed me up. The door to the private apartments with the big red heart on it was unlocked, so I knocked and walked straight in.

The Queen of Hearts was alone, standing in front

of the mirror, holding a plate of jam tarts with one hand, powdering her nose with the other. She turned, saw me, and gasped, dropping the tarts.

"Hey, Queenie," I said. "Or would you feel more comfortable if I called you Jill?"

She was still a good-looking slice of dame, even without the blonde wig.

"Get out of here!" she hissed.

"I don't think so, toots." I sat down on the bed. "Let me spell a few things out for you."

"Go ahead." She reached behind her for a concealed alarm button. I let her press it. I'd cut the wires on my way in—in my profession there's no such thing as being too careful.

"Let me spell a few things out for you."

"You just said that."

"I'll tell this my way, lady."

I lit a cigarette, and a thin plume of blue smoke drifted heavenward, which was where I was going if my hunch was wrong. Still, I've learned to trust hunches.

"Try this on for size. Dumpty—the Fat Man—wasn't your brother. He wasn't even your friend. In fact he was blackmailing you. He knew about your nose."

She turned whiter than a number of corpses I've met in my time in the business. Her hand reached up and cradled her freshly powdered nose.

"You see, I've known the Fat Man for many years, and many years ago he had a lucrative concern in training animals and birds to do certain unsavory things. And that got me to thinking. . . . I had a client recently who didn't show, due to his having been stiffed first. Dr. Foster, of Gloucester, the plastic surgeon. The official version of his death was that he'd just sat too close to a fire and melted.

"But just suppose he was killed to stop him telling something that he knew. I put two and two together and hit the jackpot. Let me reconstruct a scene for you: You were out in the garden—probably hanging out some clothes—when along came one of Dumpty's trained pie blackbirds and *pecked off your nose.*

"So there you were, standing in the garden, your hand in front of your face, when along came the Fat Man with an offer you couldn't refuse. He could introduce you to a plastic surgeon who could fix you up with a nose as good as new, for a price. And no one need ever know. Am I right so far?"

She nodded dumbly, then, finding her voice, muttered, "Pretty much. But I ran back into the parlor after the attack, to eat some bread and honey. That was where he found me."

"Fair enough." The color was starting to come back into her cheeks now. "So you had the operation from Foster, and no one was going to be any the wiser. Until Dumpty told you that he had photos of the op. You had to get rid of him. A couple of days later you were out walking in the palace grounds. There was Humpty, sitting on a wall, his back to you, gazing out into the distance. In a fit of madness, you pushed. And Humpty Dumpty had a great fall.

"But now you were in big trouble. Nobody suspected you of his murder, but where were the photographs? Foster didn't have them, although he smelled a rat and had to be disposed of—before he could see me. But you didn't know how much he'd told me, and you still didn't have the snapshots, so you took me on to find out. And that was your mistake, sister."

Her lower lip trembled, and my heart quivered. "You won't turn me in, will you?"

"Sister, you tried to frame me this afternoon. I don't take kindly to that."

With a shaking hand she started to unbutton the top button of her blouse. "Perhaps we could come to some sort of arrangement?"

I shook my head. "Sorry, your majesty. Mrs. Horner's little boy Jack was always taught to keep his hands off royalty. It's a pity, but that's how it is." To be on the safe side I looked away, which was a mistake. A cute little ladies' pistol was in her hands and pointing at me before you could sing a song of sixpence. The shooter may have been small, but I knew it packed enough of a wallop to take me out of the game permanently.

This dame was *lethal*.

"Put that gun down, your majesty." Sergeant O'Grady strolled through the bedroom door, his police special clutched in his hamlike fist.

"I'm sorry I suspected you, Horner," he said drily. "You're lucky I did, though, sure and begorrah. I had you tailed here and I overheard the whole thing."

"Hi, Sarge, thanks for stopping by. But I hadn't finished my explanation. If you'll take a seat I'll wrap it up."

He nodded brusquely, and sat down near the door. His gun hardly moved.

I got up from the bed and walked over to the Queen. "You see, toots, what I didn't tell you was who *did* have the snaps of your nose job. Humpty did, when you killed him."

A charming frown crinkled her perfect brow. "I don't understand. . . . I had the body searched."

"Sure, afterward. But the first people to get to the Fat Man were the King's Men. The cops. And one of them pocketed the envelope. When any fuss had died down the blackmail would have started again. Only this time you wouldn't have known who to kill. And I owe you an apology." I bent down to tie my shoelaces.

"Why?"

"I accused you of trying to frame me this afternoon. You didn't. That arrow was the property of a boy who was the best archer in my school—I should have recognized that distinctive fletching anywhere. Isn't that right," I said, turning back to the door, "'Sparrow' O'Grady?"

Under the guise of tying my shoelaces I had already palmed a couple of the Queen's jam tarts, and, flinging one of them upward, I neatly smashed the room's only lightbulb.

It only delayed the shooting a few seconds, but a few seconds was all I needed, and as the Queen of Hearts and Sergeant "Sparrow" O'Grady cheerfully shot each other to bits, I split.

In my business, you have to look after number one.

Munching on a jam tart I walked out of the palace grounds and into the street. I paused by a trash can, to try to burn the manila envelope of photographs I had pulled from O'Grady's pocket as I walked past him, but it was raining so hard they wouldn't catch.

When I got back to my office I phoned the tourist board to complain. They said the rain was good for the farmers, and I told them what they could do with it.

They said that things are tough all over.

And I said, "Yeah."

Troll Bridge

THEY PULLED UP MOST of the railway tracks in
the early sixties, when I was three or four.
They slashed the train services to ribbons.
This meant that there was nowhere to go but
London, and the little town where I lived became
the end of the line.

My earliest reliable memory: eighteen months
old, my mother away in hospital having my sister,
and my grandmother walking with me down to a
bridge, and lifting me up to watch the train below,
panting and steaming like a black iron dragon.

Over the next few years they lost the last of the
steam trains, and with them went the network of
railways that joined village to village, town to town.

I didn't know that the trains were going. By the
time I was seven they were a thing of the past.

We lived in an old house on the outskirts of the
town. The fields opposite were empty and fallow. I

used to climb the fence and lie in the shade of a small bulrush patch, and read; or if I were feeling more adventurous I'd explore the grounds of the empty manor beyond the fields. It had a weed-clogged ornamental pond, with a low wooden bridge over it. I never saw any groundsmen or caretakers in my forays through the gardens and woods, and I never attempted to enter the manor. That would have been courting disaster, and, besides, it was a matter of faith for me that all empty old houses were haunted.

It is not that I was credulous, simply that I believed in all things dark and dangerous. It was part of my young creed that the night was full of ghosts and witches, hungry and flapping and dressed completely in black.

The converse held reassuringly true: daylight was safe. Daylight was always safe.

A ritual: on the last day of the summer school term, walking home from school, I would remove my shoes and socks and, carrying them in my hands, walk down the stony flinty lane on pink and tender feet. During the summer holiday I would put shoes on only under duress. I would revel in my freedom from footwear until school term began once more in September.

When I was seven I discovered the path through the wood. It was summer, hot and bright, and I wandered a long way from home that day.

I was exploring. I went past the manor, its windows boarded up and blind, across the grounds, and through some unfamiliar woods. I scrambled down a steep bank, and I found myself on a shady path that was new to me and overgrown with trees; the light that penetrated the leaves was stained green and gold, and I thought I was in fairyland.

A little stream trickled down the side of the path, teeming with tiny, transparent shrimps. I picked them up and watched them jerk and spin on my fingertips. Then I put them back.

I wandered down the path. It was perfectly straight, and overgrown with short grass. From time to time I would find these really terrific rocks: bubbly, melted things, brown and purple and black. If you held them up to the light you could see every color of the rainbow. I was convinced that they had to be extremely valuable, and stuffed my pockets with them.

I walked and walked down the quiet golden-green corridor, and saw nobody.

I wasn't hungry or thirsty. I just wondered where the path was going. It traveled in a straight line, and was perfectly flat. The path never changed, but the countryside around it did. At first I was walking along the bottom of a ravine, grassy banks climbing steeply on each side of me. Later, the path was above everything, and as I walked I could look down at the treetops below me, and the roofs of the occasional distant houses. My path was always flat and straight, and I walked along it through valleys and plateaus, valleys and plateaus. And eventually, in one of the valleys, I came to the bridge.

It was built of clean red brick, a huge curving arch over the path. At the side of the bridge were stone steps cut into the embankment, and, at the top of the steps, a little wooden gate.

I was surprised to see any token of the existence of humanity on my path, which I was by now convinced was a natural formation, like a volcano. And, with a sense more of curiosity than anything else (I had, after all, walked hundreds of miles, or so I was convinced, and might be *anywhere*), I climbed the stone steps, and went through the gate.

I was nowhere.

The top of the bridge was paved with mud. On each side of it was a meadow. The meadow on my side was a wheatfield; the other field was just grass. There were the caked imprints of huge tractor wheels in the dried mud. I walked across the bridge to be sure: no trip-trap, my bare feet were soundless.

Nothing for miles; just fields and wheat and trees.

I picked a stalk of wheat, and pulled out the sweet grains, peeling them between my fingers, chewing them meditatively.

I realized then that I was getting hungry, and went back down the stairs to the abandoned railway track. It was time to go home. I was not lost; all I needed to do was follow my path home once more.

There was a troll waiting for me, under the bridge.

"I'm a troll," he said. Then he paused, and added, more or less as an afterthought, "Fol rol de ol rol."

He was huge: his head brushed the top of the brick arch. He was more or less translucent: I could see the bricks and trees behind him, dimmed but not lost. He was all my nightmares given flesh. He had huge strong teeth, and rending claws, and

strong, hairy hands. His hair was long, like one of my sister's little plastic gonks, and his eyes bulged. He was naked, and his penis hung from the bush of gonk hair between his legs.

"I heard you, Jack," he whispered, in a voice like the wind. "I heard you trip-trapping over my bridge. And now I'm going to eat your life."

I was only seven, but it was daylight, and I do not remember being scared. It is good for children to find themselves facing the elements of a fairy tale— they are well-equipped to deal with these.

"Don't eat me," I said to the troll. I was wearing a stripy brown T-shirt and brown corduroy trousers. My hair also was brown, and I was missing a front tooth. I was learning to whistle between my teeth, but wasn't there yet.

"I'm going to eat your life, Jack," said the troll.

I stared the troll in the face. "My big sister is going to be coming down the path soon," I lied, "and she's far tastier than me. Eat her instead."

The troll sniffed the air, and smiled. "You're all alone," he said. "There's nothing else on the path. Nothing at all." Then he leaned down, and ran his fingers over me: it felt like butterflies were brushing my face—like the touch of a blind person. Then he snuffled his fingers, and shook his huge head. "You don't have a big sister. You've only a younger sister, and she's at her friend's today."

"Can you tell all that from smell?" I asked, amazed.

"Trolls can smell the rainbows, trolls can smell the stars," it whispered, sadly. "Trolls can smell the dreams you dreamed before you were ever born. Come close to me and I'll eat your life."

"I've got precious stones in my pocket," I told the troll. "Take them, not me. Look." I showed him the lava jewel rocks I had found earlier.

"Clinker," said the troll. "The discarded refuse of steam trains. Of no value to me."

He opened his mouth wide. Sharp teeth. Breath that smelled of leaf mold and the underneaths of things. "Eat. Now."

He became more and more solid to me, more and more real; and the world outside became flatter, began to fade.

"Wait." I dug my feet into the damp earth beneath the bridge, wiggled my toes, held on tightly to the real world. I stared into his big eyes. "You don't want to eat my life. Not yet. I—I'm only seven. I haven't *lived* at all yet. There are books I haven't read yet. I've never been on an airplane. I can't whistle yet—not really. Why don't you let me go? When I'm older and bigger and more of a meal I'll come back to you."

The troll stared at me with eyes like headlamps. Then it nodded.

"When you come back, then," it said. And it smiled.

I turned around and walked back down the silent straight path where the railway lines had once been.

After a while I began to run.

I pounded down the track in the green light, puffing and blowing, until I felt a stabbing ache beneath my rib cage, the pain of stitch; and, clutching my side, I stumbled home.

The fields started to go, as I grew older. One by one, row by row, houses sprang up with roads named after wildflowers and respectable authors. Our home—an aging, tattered Victorian house—was sold, and torn down; new houses covered the garden.

They built houses everywhere.

I once got lost in the new housing estate that

covered two meadows I had once known every inch of. I didn't mind too much that the fields were going, though. The old manor house was bought by a multinational, and the grounds became more houses.

It was eight years before I returned to the old railway line, and when I did, I was not alone.

I was fifteen; I'd changed schools twice in that time. Her name was Louise, and she was my first love.

I loved her gray eyes, and her fine light brown hair, and her gawky way of walking (like a fawn just learning to walk which sounds really dumb, for which I apologize): I saw her chewing gum, when I was thirteen, and I fell for her like a suicide from a bridge.

The main trouble with being in love with Louise was that we were best friends, and we were both going out with other people.

I'd never told her I loved her, or even that I fancied her. We were buddies.

I'd been at her house that evening: we sat in her room and played *Rattus Norvegicus*, the first Stranglers LP. It was the beginning of punk, and everything seemed so exciting: the possibilities, in music as in everything else, were endless. Eventually it was time for me to go home, and she decided to accompany me. We held hands, innocently, just pals, and we strolled the ten-minute walk to my house.

The moon was bright, and the world was visible and colorless, and the night was warm.

We got to my house. Saw the lights inside, and stood in the driveway, and talked about the band I was starting. We didn't go in.

Then it was decided that I'd walk *her* home. So we walked back to her house.

She told me about the battles she was having with her younger sister, who was stealing her makeup and perfume. Louise suspected that her sister was having sex with boys. Louise was a virgin. We both were.

We stood in the road outside her house, under the sodium-yellow streetlight, and we stared at each other's black lips and pale yellow faces.

We grinned at each other.

Then we just walked, picking quiet roads and empty paths. In one of the new housing estates, a path led us into the woodland, and we followed it.

The path was straight and dark, but the lights of

distant houses shone like stars on the ground, and the moon gave us enough light to see. Once we were scared, when something snuffled and snorted in front of us. We pressed close, saw it was a badger, laughed and hugged and kept on walking.

We talked quiet nonsense about what we dreamed and wanted and thought.

And all the time I wanted to kiss her and feel her breasts, and hold her, and be held by her.

Finally I saw my chance. There was an old brick bridge over the path, and we stopped beneath it. I pressed up against her. Her mouth opened against mine.

Then she went cold and stiff, and stopped moving.

"Hello," said the troll.

I let go of Louise. It was dark beneath the bridge, but the shape of the troll filled the darkness.

"I froze her," said the troll, "so we can talk. Now: I'm going to eat your life."

My heart pounded, and I could feel myself trembling.

"No."

"You said you'd come back to me. And you have. Did you learn to whistle?"

35

"Yes."

"That's good. I never could whistle." It sniffed, and nodded. "I am pleased. You have grown in life and experience. More to eat. More for me."

I grabbed Louise, a taut zombie, and pushed her forward. "Don't take me. I don't want to die. Take *her*. I bet she's much tastier than me. And she's two months older than I am. Why don't you take her?"

The troll was silent.

It sniffed Louise from toe to head, snuffling at her feet and crotch and breasts and hair.

Then it looked at me.

"She's an innocent," it said. "You're not. I don't want her. I want you."

I walked to the opening of the bridge and stared up at the stars in the night.

"But there's so much I've never done," I said, partly to myself. "I mean, I've never. Well, I've never had sex. And I've never been to America. I haven't . . ." I paused. " I haven't *done* anything. Not yet."

The troll said nothing.

"I could come back to you. When I'm older."

The troll said nothing.

"I *will* come back. Honest I will."

"Come back to me?" said Louise. "Why? Where are you going?"

I turned around. The troll had gone, and the girl I had thought I loved was standing in the shadows beneath the bridge.

"We're going home," I told her. "Come on."

We walked back, and never said anything.

She went out with the drummer in the punk band I started, and, much later, married someone else. We met once, on a train, after she was married, and she asked me if I remembered that night.

I said I did.

"I really liked you, that night, Jack," she told me. "I thought you were going to kiss me. I thought you were going to ask me out. I would have said yes. If you had."

"But I didn't."

"No," she said. "You didn't." Her hair was cut very short. It didn't suit her.

I never saw her again. The trim woman with the taut smile was not the girl I had loved, and talking to her made me feel uncomfortable.

I moved to London, and then, some years later, I moved back again, but the town I returned to was not the town I remembered: there were no fields, no farms, no little flint lanes; and I moved away as soon as I could, to a tiny village ten miles down the road.

I moved with my family—I was married by now, with a toddler—into an old house that had once, many years before, been a railway station. The tracks had been dug up, and the old couple who lived opposite us used the ground where the tracks had been to grow vegetables.

I was getting older. One day I found a gray hair; on another, I heard a recording of myself talking, and I realized I sounded just like my father.

I was working in London, doing A&R for one of the major record companies. I was commuting into London by train most days, coming back some evenings.

I had to keep a small flat in London; it's hard to commute when the bands you're checking out don't even stagger onto the stage until midnight. It also meant that it was fairly easy to get laid, if I wanted to, which I did.

I thought that Eleanora—that was my wife's name; I should have mentioned that before, I suppose—didn't know about the other women; but I got back from a two-week jaunt to New York one winter's day, and when I arrived at the house it was empty and cold.

She had left a letter, not a note. Fifteen pages, neatly typed, and every word of it was true. Including the PS, which read: *You really don't love me. And you never did.*

I put on a heavy coat, and I left the house and just walked, stunned and slightly numb.

There was no snow on the ground, but there was a hard frost, and the leaves crunched under my feet as I walked. The trees were skeletal black against the harsh gray winter sky.

I walked down the side of the road. Cars passed me, traveling to and from London. Once I tripped on a branch, half hidden in a heap of brown leaves, ripping my trousers, cutting my leg.

I reached the next village. There was a river at right angles to the road, and a path I'd never seen before beside it, and I walked down the path, and stared at the partly frozen river. It gurgled and plashed and sang.

The path led off through fields; it was straight and grassy.

I found a rock, half buried, on one side of the path. I picked it up, brushed off the mud. It was a melted lump of purplish stuff, with a strange rainbow sheen to it. I put it into the pocket of my coat and held it in my hand as I walked, its presence warm and reassuring.

The river meandered away across the fields, and I walked on in silence.

I had walked for an hour before I saw houses—new and small and square—on the embankment above me.

And then I saw the bridge, and I knew where I was: I was on the old railway path, and I'd been coming down it from the other direction.

There were graffiti painted on the side of the bridge: BARRY LOVES SUSAN and the omnipresent NF of the National Front.

I stood beneath the bridge in the red brick arch, stood among the ice-cream wrappers, and the crisp packets, and watched my breath steam in the cold afternoon air.

The blood had dried into my trousers.

Cars passed over the bridge above me; I could hear a radio playing loudly in one of them.

"Hello?" I said quietly, feeling embarrassed, feeling foolish. "Hello?"

There was no answer. The wind rustled the crisp packets and the leaves.

"I came back. I said I would. And I did. Hello?"

Silence.

I began to cry then, stupidly, silently, sobbing under the bridge.

A hand touched my face, and I looked up.

"I didn't think you'd come back," said the troll.

He was my height now, but otherwise unchanged. His long gonk hair was unkempt and had leaves in it, and his eyes were wide and lonely.

I shrugged, then wiped my face with the sleeve of my coat. "I came back."

Three kids passed above us on the bridge, shouting and running.

"I'm a troll," whispered the troll in a small, scared voice. "Fol rol de ol rol."

He was trembling.

I held out my hand and took his huge clawed paw in mine. I smiled at him. "It's okay," I told him. "Honestly. It's okay."

The troll nodded.

He pushed me to the ground, onto the leaves and the wrappers, and lowered himself on top of me. Then he raised his head, and opened his mouth, and ate my life with his strong sharp teeth.

When he was finished, the troll stood up and brushed himself down. He put his hand into the pocket of his coat and pulled out a bubbly, burnt lump of clinker rock.

He held it out to me.

"This is yours," said the troll.

I looked at him: wearing my life comfortably, easily, as if he'd been wearing it for years. I took the clinker from his hand, and sniffed it. I could smell the train from which it had fallen, so long ago. I gripped it tightly in my hairy hand.

"Thank you," I said.

"Good luck," said the troll.

"Yeah. Well. You too."

The troll grinned with my face.

It turned its back on me and began to walk back the way I had come, toward the village, back to the empty house I had left that morning; and it whistled as it walked.

I've been here ever since. Hiding. Waiting. Part of the bridge.

I watch from the shadows as the people pass: walking their dogs, or talking, or doing the things that people do. Sometimes people pause beneath my bridge, to stand, or piss, or make love. And I watch them, but say nothing; and they never see me.

Fol rol de ol rol.

I'm just going to stay here, in the darkness under the arch. I can hear you all out there, trip-trapping, trip-trapping over my bridge.

Oh yes, I can hear you.

But I'm not coming out.

Don't Ask Jack

NOBODY KNEW WHERE THE toy had come from, which great-grandparent or distant aunt had owned it before it was given to the nursery.

It was a box, carved and painted in gold and red. It was undoubtedly attractive and, or so the grown-ups maintained, quite valuable—perhaps even an antique. The latch, unfortunately, was rusted shut, and the key had been lost, so the Jack could not be released from his box. Still, it was a remarkable box, heavy and carved and gilt.

The children did not play with it. It sat at the bottom of the huge old wooden toy box, which was the same size and age as a pirate's treasure chest, or so the children thought. The Jack-in-the-Box was buried beneath dolls and trains, clowns and paper stars and old conjuring tricks, and crippled marionettes with their strings irrevocably tangled, with dressing-up clothes (here the tatters of a long-ago wedding dress, there a black silk hat crusted with age and time) and costume jewelry, broken hoops and tops and hobbyhorses. Under them all was Jack's box.

The children did not play with it. They whispered among themselves, alone in the attic nursery. On gray days when the wind howled about the house and rain rattled the slates and pattered down the eaves they told each other stories about Jack, although they had never seen him. One claimed that Jack was an evil wizard, placed in the box as punishment for crimes too awful to describe; another (I am certain that it must have been one of the girls) maintained that Jack's box was Pandora's box, and he had been placed in the box as guardian to prevent the bad things inside it from coming out once more. They would not even touch the box, if they could help it, although when, as happened from time to time, an adult would comment on the absence of that sweet old Jack-in-the-Box, and retrieve it from the chest, and place it in a position of honor on the mantelpiece, then the children would pluck up their courage and, later, hide it away once more in the darkness.

The children did not play with the Jack-in-the-Box. And when they grew up and left the great house, the attic nursery was closed up and almost forgotten.

Almost, but not entirely. For each of the children, separately, remembered walking alone in the moon's blue light, on his or her own bare feet, up to the nursery. It was almost like sleepwalking, feet soundless on the wood of the stairs, on the threadbare nursery carpet. Remembered opening the treasure chest, pawing through the dolls and the clothes and pulling out the box.

And then the child would touch the catch, and the lid would open, slow as a sunset, and the music would begin to play, and Jack came out. Not with a pop and a bounce: he was no spring-heeled Jack. But deliberately, intently, he would rise from the box and motion to the child to come closer, closer, and smile.

And there in the moonlight, he told them each things they could never quite remember, things they were never able entirely to forget.

The oldest boy died in the Great War. The

youngest, after their parents died, inherited the house, although it was taken from him when he was found in the cellar one night with cloths and paraffin and matches, trying to burn the great house to the ground. They took him to the madhouse, and perhaps he is there still.

The other children, who had once been girls and now were women, declined, each and every one, to return to the house in which they had grown up; and the windows of the house were boarded up, and the doors were all locked with huge iron keys, and the sisters visited it as often as they visited their eldest brother's grave, or the sad thing that had once been their younger brother, which is to say, never.

Years have passed, and the girls are old women, and owls and bats have made their homes in the old attic nursery; rats build their nests among the forgotten toys. The creatures gaze uncuriously at the faded prints on the wall, and stain the remnants of the carpet with their droppings.

And deep within the box within the box, Jack waits and smiles, holding his secrets. He is waiting for the children. He can wait forever.

How to Sell the Ponti Bridge

MY FAVORITE ROGUES' CLUB is the oldest and still the most exclusive in all the Seven Worlds. It was formed by a loose association of rogues, cheats, scoundrels, and confidence men almost seventy thousand years ago. It has been copied many times in many places (there was one started quite recently, within the last five hundred years at any rate, in the City of London), but none of the other clubs matches the original Rogues' Club, in the city of Lost Carnadine, for atmosphere. No other club has quite so select a membership.

And the membership of the Lost Carnadine Rogues' Club is particularly select. You will understand the kind of person who makes it to membership if I tell you that I myself have seen, walking or sitting or eating or talking, in its many rooms, such notables as Daraxius Lo (who sold the Kzem a frog-bat on a holy day), Prottle (who sold the palace of the King of Vandaria to the King of Vandaria), and the self-styled Lord Niff (who, I have heard it whispered, was the original inventor of the fox twist, the cheat that broke the bank at the Casino Grande). In addition, I have seen Rogues of interuniversal renown fail to gain admittance to even discuss their membership with the secretary—on one memorable day I passed a famous financier, in company with the head of the Hy-Brasail mafia and a preeminent prime minister on their way down the back stairs with the blackest of expressions upon their faces, having obviously been told not even to think about returning. No, the ones who make it into the Rogues' Club are a high bunch. I am sure that you will have heard of each of them. Not under those names, of course, but the touch is distinctive, is it not?

I myself gained membership by means of a brilliant piece of creative scientific research, something that revolutionized the thinking of a whole generation. It was my disdain for regular methodology and, as I have said, creative research that gained me membership, and when I am in that part of the cosmos I make a point of stopping off for an evening, taking in some sparkling conversation, drinking the club's fine wines, and basking in the presence of my moral equals.

It was late in the evening and the log fire was burning low in the grate, and a handful of us sat and drank one of the fine dark wines of Spidireen in an alcove in the great hall. "Of course," one of my new friends was saying, "there are some scams that no self-respecting rogue would ever touch, they are so old and classless and tired. For example, selling a tourist the Ponti Bridge."

"It's the same with Nelson's Column, or the Eiffel Tower, or the Brooklyn Bridge, back on my home-world," I told them. "Sad little con games, with as much class as a back-alley game of Find the Lady. But look on the good side: Nobody who sold the Ponti Bridge would ever get membership in a club like this."

"No?" said a quiet voice from the corner of the room. "How strange. I do believe it was the time I sold the Ponti Bridge that gained me membership in this club." A tall gentleman, quite bald and most exquisitely dressed, got up from the chair in which he had been sitting, and walked over to us. He was sipping the inside of an imported rhûm fruit, and smiling, I think at the effect that he had created. He walked over to us, pulled up a cushion, and sat down. "I don't believe we've met," he said.

My friends introduced themselves (the gray-haired deft woman, Gloathis; the short, quiet dodger Redcap) as did I.

He smiled wider. "Your fame precedes each of you. I am honored. You may call me Stoat."

"Stoat?" said Gloathis. "The only Stoat I ever heard of was the man who pulled the Derana Kite job, but that was . . . what, over a hundred years ago. What am I thinking? You adopted the name as a tribute, I presume."

"You are a wise woman," said Stoat. "It would be impossible for me to be the same man." He leaned forward on his cushion. "You were talking about the sale of the Ponti Bridge?"

"Indeed we were."

"And you were all of the opinion that selling the Ponti Bridge is a measly scam, unworthy of a member of this club? And perhaps you are right. Let us examine the ingredients of a good scam." He ticked off the points on the fingers of his left hand as he spoke. "*Firstly,* the scam must be credible. *Secondly,* it must be simple—the more complex the more chance of error. *Thirdly,* when the sucker is stung he must be stung in such a way as to prevent him from ever turning to the law. *Fourthly,* the mainspring of any elegant con is human greed and human vanity. *Lastly,* it must involve trust—confidence, if you will."

"Surely," said Gloathis.

"So you are telling me that the sale of the Ponti Bridge—or any other major landmark not yours to sell—cannot have these characteristics? Gentlemen. Lady. Let me tell you my story.

"I had arrived in Ponti some years ago almost penniless. I had but thirty gold crowns, and I needed a million. Why? I am afraid that is another story. I took stock of myself—I had the gold crowns and some smart robes. I was fluent in the aristocratic Ponti dialect, and I am, I pride myself, quite brilliant. Still, I could think of nothing that would bring me the kind of money I had to have in the time by which I needed it. My mind, usually teeming and coruscating with fine schemes, was a perfect blank. So, trusting to my gods to bring me inspiration, I went on a guided tour of the city. . . ."

Ponti lies to the south and to the east, a free city and port at the foot of the Mountains of Dawn. Ponti is a sprawling city, on either side of the Bay of Dawn, a beautiful natural harbor. Spanning the bay is the bridge, which was built of jewels, of mortar, and of magic nearly two thousand years ago. There were jeers when it was first planned and begun, for none credited that a structure almost half a mile across could ever be successfully completed, or would stand for long once erected, but the bridge was completed, and the jeers turned to gasps of awe and civic pride. It spanned the Bay of Dawn, a perfect structure that flashed and shone and glinted in myriad rainbow colors beneath the noon sun.

The tour guide paused at the foot of it. "As you can see, ladies and gentlemen, if you will examine closely, the bridge is built entirely of precious stones—rubies, diamonds, sapphires, emeralds, chryolanths, carbuncles, and such—and they are bound together with a transparent mortar which was crafted by the twin sages Hrolgar and Hrylthfgur out of a primal magic. The jewels are all real—make no mistake about that—and were gathered from all five corners of the world by Emmidus, King of Ponti at the time."

A small boy near the front of the group turned to his mother and announced loudly, "We did him in school. He's called Emmidus the Last, because there weren't any more after him. And they told us—"

The tour guide interrupted smoothly. "The young man is quite correct. King Emmidus bankrupted the city-state obtaining the jewels, and thus set the scene for our current beneficent Ruling Enclave to appear."

The small boy's mother was now twisting his ear, which cheered the tour guide up immensely. "I'm sure you've heard that confidence tricksters are always trying to play tourists for mugs by telling them that they are representing the Ruling Enclave, and that as the owners of the bridge they are entitled to sell it. They get a hefty deposit, then scarper. To clarify matters," he said, as he said five times each day, and he and the tourists chuckled together, "the bridge is definitely not for sale." It was a good line. It always got a laugh.

His party started to make its way across the

bridge. Only the small boy noticed that one of their number had remained behind—a tall man, quite bald. He stood at the foot of the bridge, lost in contemplation. The boy wanted to point this out to everybody, but his ear hurt, and so he said nothing.

The man at the foot of the bridge smiled abruptly. "Not for sale, eh?" he said aloud. Then he turned and walked back to the city.

They were playing a game not unlike tennis with large heavy-strung racquets and jeweled skulls for balls. The skulls were so *satisfying* in the way they *thunked* when hit cleanly, in the way they curved in great looping parabolas across the marble court. The skulls had never sat on human necks; they had been obtained, at great loss of life and significant expense, from a demon race in the highlands, and, afterward jeweled (emeralds and sweet rubies set in a lacy silver filigree in the eye sockets and about the jawbone) in Carthus's own workshops.

It was Carthus's serve.

He reached for the next skull in the pile and held it up to the light, marveling at the craftsmanship, in the way that the jewels, when struck by the light at a certain angle, seemed to glow with an inner luminescence. He could have told you the exact value and the probable provenance of each jewel—perhaps the very mine from which it had been dug. The skulls were also beautiful: bone the color of milky mother-of-pearl, translucent and fine. Each had cost him more than the value of the jewels set in its elegant bony face. The demon race had now been hunted to the verge of extinction, and the skulls were well-nigh irreplaceable.

He lobbed the skull over the net. Aathia struck it neatly back at him, forcing him to run to meet it (his footsteps echoing on the cold marble floor) and—*thunk*—hit it back to her.

She almost reached it in time. Almost, but not quite: the skull eluded her racquet and fell toward the stone floor and then, only an inch or so above the ground, it stopped, bobbing slightly, as if immersed in liquid or a magnetic field.

It was magic, of course, and Carthus had paid most highly for it. He could afford to.

"My point, lady," he called, bowing low.

Aathia—his partner in all but love—said nothing. Her eyes glinted like chips of ice, or like the jewels that were the only things she loved. Carthus and Aathia, jewel merchants. They made a strange pair.

There was a discreet cough from behind Carthus. He turned to see a white-tuniced slave holding a parchment scroll. "Yes?" said Carthus. He wiped the sweat from his face with the back of his hand.

"A message, lord. The man who left it said that it was urgent."

Carthus grunted. "Who's it from?"

"I have not opened it. I was told it was for your eyes and the eyes of the Lady Aathia, and for no other."

Carthus stared at the parchment scroll but made no move to take it. He was a big man with a fleshy face, sandy receding hair, and a worried expression. His business rivals—and there were many, for Ponti had become, over the years, the center of the wholesale jewel business—had learned that his expression held no clue to his inner feelings. In many cases it had cost them money to learn this.

"Take the message, Carthus," said Aathia, and when he did not, she walked around the net herself and plucked the scroll from the slave's fingers. "Leave us."

The slave's bare feet were soundless on the chill marble floor.

Aathia broke the seal with her sleeve knife and unrolled the parchment. Her eyes flicked over it once, fast, then again at a slower pace. She whistled. "Here . . ." Carthus took it and read it through.

"I—I really don't know what to make of it," he said in a high, petulant voice. With his racquet he rubbed absentmindedly at the small crisscross scar on his right cheek. The pendant that hung about his neck, proclaiming him one of the High Council of the Ponti Jewel Merchants' Guild, stuck briefly to his sweaty skin, and then swung free. "What do you think, my flower?"

"I am not your 'flower.'"

"Of course not, lady."

"Better, Carthus. We'll make a real citizen of you yet. Well, for a start, the name is obviously false. 'Glew Croll' indeed! There are more men named Glew Croll in Ponti than there are diamonds in your storehouses. The address is obviously rented accommodation in the Undercliffs. There was no ring mark on the wax seal. It's as if he has gone out of his way to maintain anonymity."

"Yes. I can see all that. But what about this 'business opportunity' he talks about? And if it is, as he implies, Ruling Enclave business, why would it be carried on with the secrecy he requests?"

She shrugged. "The Ruling Enclave has never been averse to secrecy. And, reading between the lines, it would appear that there is a great deal of wealth involved."

Carthus was silent. He reached down to the skull pile, leaned his racquet against it, and placed the scroll beside it. He picked up a large skull. He caressed it gently with his blunt, stubby fingers. "You know," he said, as if speaking to the skull, "this could be my chance to get one up on the the rest of the bleeders on the Guild High Council. Dead-blood aristocratic half-wits."

"There speaks the son of a slave," said Aathia. "If it wasn't for my name you would never have made council membership."

"Shut up." His expression was vaguely worried, which meant nothing at all. "I can show them. I'm going to show them. You'll see."

He hefted the skull in his right hand as if testing the weight of it, reveling in and computing the value of the bone, the jewels, the fine-worked silver. Then he spun around, suprisingly fast for one so big, and threw the skull with all his might at a far pillar, well beyond the field of play. It seemed to hang in the air forever and then, with a painful slowness, it hit the pillar and smashed into a thousand fragments. The almost-musical tinkling sounds it made as it did so were very beautiful.

"I'll go and change and meet this Glew Croll then," muttered Carthus. He walked out of the room, carrying the scroll with him. Aathia stared at him as he left, then she clapped her hands, summoning a slave to clear up the mess.

The caves that honeycomb the rock on the north side of the Bay of Dawn, down into the bay, beneath the bridge, are known as the Undercliffs. Carthus took his clothes off at the door, handing them to his slave, and walked down the narrow stone steps. His flesh gave an involuntary shiver as he entered the water (kept a little below blood temperature in the aristocratic manner, but still chill after the heat of the day), and he swam down the corridor into an anteroom. Reflected light glimmered across the walls. On the water floated four other men and two women. They lounged on large wooden floats, elegantly carved into the shapes of waterbirds and fish.

Carthus swam over to an empty float—a dolphin—and hauled his bulk up onto it. Like the other six he wore nothing but the Jewelers' Guild High Council pendant. All the High Council members, bar one, were there.

"Where's the president?" he asked of no one in particular.

A skeletal woman with flawless white skin pointed to one of the inner rooms. Then she yawned and twisted her body, a rippling twist, at the end of which she was off the float—hers was carved into the shape of a giant swan—and into the water. Carthus envied and hated her: that twist had been one of the twelve so-called noble dives. He knew that, despite having practiced for years, he could not hope to emulate her.

"Effete bitch," he muttered beneath his breath. Still, it was reassuring to see other council members here. He wondered if any of them knew anything he didn't.

There was a splashing behind him, and he turned. Wommet, the council president, was clutching

Carthus's float. They bowed to each other, then Wommet (a small hunchback, whose ever so many times great-grandfather had made his fortune finding for King Emmidus the jewels that had bankrupted Ponti, and had thus laid the foundations for the Ruling Enclave's two-thousand-year rule) said, "He will speak to you next, Messire Carthus. Down the corridor on the left. It's the first room you come to."

The other council members, on their floats, looked at Carthus blankly. They were aristocrats of Ponti, and so they hid their envy and their irritation that Carthus was going in before them, although they did not hide it as well as they thought they did; and, somewhere deep inside, Carthus smiled.

He suppressed the urge to ask the hunchback what this business was all about, and he slipped off his float. The warmed seawater stung his eyes.

The room in which Grew Croll waited was up several rock steps, and was dry and dark and smoky. One lamp burned fitfully on the table in the center of the room. There was a robe on the chair, and Carthus slipped it on. A man stood in the shadows beyond the lamplight, but even in the murk Carthus could see that he was tall and completely bald.

"I bid you good day," said a cultured voice.

"And on your house and kin also," responded Carthus.

"Sit down, sit down. As you have undoubtedly inferred from the message I sent you, this is Ruling Enclave business. Now, before another word is said, I must ask you to read and sign this oath of secrecy. Take all the time you need." He pushed a paper across the table: it was a comprehensive oath, pledging Carthus to secrecy about all matters discussed during their meeting on pain of the Ruling Enclave's "extreme displeasure"—a polite euphemism for death. Carthus read it over twice. "It—it isn't anything illegal, is it?"

"Sir!" The cultured voice was offended. Carthus shrugged his great shoulders and signed. The paper was taken from his fingers and placed in a trunk at the far end of the hall. "Very good. We can get down to business then. Something to drink? Smoke? Inhale? No? Very well."

A pause.

"As you may have already surmised, Glew Croll is not my name. I am a junior administrative member of the Ruling Enclave." (Carthus grunted, his suspicions confirmed, and he scratched his ear.) "Messire Carthus, what do you know of the Bridge of Ponti?"

"Same as everyone. National landmark. Tourist attraction. Very impressive if you like that sort of thing. Built of jewels and magic. Jewels aren't all of the highest quality, although there's a rose diamond at the summit as big as a baby's fist, and reportedly flawless. . . ."

"Very good. Have you heard the term 'magical half-life'?"

Carthus hadn't. Not that he could recall. "I've heard the term," he said, "but I'm not a magician, obviously, and . . ."

"A magical half-life, messire, is the nigromantic term for the length of time a magician, warlock, witch, or whatever's magic lasts after his or her death. A simple hedge witch's conjurations and so on will often vanish and be done with on the moment of her death. At the other end of the scale you have such phenomena as the Sea Serpent Sea, in which the purely magical sea serpents still frolic and bask almost nine thousand years after the execution of Cilimwai Lah, their creator."

"Right. That. Yes, I knew that."

"Good. Then you will understand the import when I tell you that the half-life of the Ponti Bridge—according to the wisest of our natural philosophers—is little more than two thousand years. Soon, perhaps very soon, messire, it will begin to crumble and collapse."

The fat jeweler gasped. "But that's terrible. If the news got around . . ." He trailed off, weighing up the implications.

"Precisely. There would be panic. Trouble. Unrest. The news cannot be allowed to leak out until we are ready, hence this secrecy."

"I think I will have that drink now, please," said Carthus.

"Very wise." The bald nobleman unstoppered a crystal flagon and poured clear blue wine into a goblet. He passed it across the table and continued. "Any jeweler—and there are only seven in Ponti and perhaps two others elsewhere who could cope with the volume—who was permitted to demolish and keep the materials of the Ponti Bridge would regain whatever he paid for it in publicity alone, leaving aside the value of the jewels. It is my task to talk to the city's most prestigious wholesale jewelers about this matter.

"The Ruling Enclave has a number of concerns. As you can imagine, if the jewels were all released at once in Ponti, they would soon be almost worthless. In exchange for entire ownership of the bridge, the jeweler would have to undertake to build a structure beneath it, and as the bridge crumbles he or she would collect the jewels, and would undertake to sell no more than half a percent of them within the city walls. You, as the senior partner in Carthus and Aathia, are one of the people I have been appointed to discuss this matter with."

The jeweler shook his head. It seemed almost too good to be true—*if* he could get it. "Anything else?" he asked. His voice was casual. He sounded uninterested.

"I am but a humble servant of the Enclave," said the bald man. "They, for their part, will wish to make a profit on this. Each of you will submit a tender for the bridge, via myself, to the Ruling Enclave. There is to be no conferring among you jewelers. The Enclave will choose the best offer and then, in open and formal session, the winner will be announced and then—and only then—will the winner pay any money into the city treasury. Most of the winning bid, as I understand things, will go toward the building of another bridge (out of significantly more mundane materials, I suspect) and to paying for a ferry for the citizens while there is no bridge."

"I see."

The tall man stared at Carthus. To the jeweler it seemed as if those hard eyes were boring into his soul. "You have exactly five days to submit your tender, Carthus. Let me warn you of two things. Firstly, if there is any indication of collaboration between any of you jewelers, you will earn the Enclave's extreme displeasure. Secondly, if *anybody* finds out about the spell fatigue, then we will not waste time in finding out which of you jewelers opened his mouth too wide and not too well. The High Council of the Ponti Jewelers' Guild will be replaced with another council, and your businesses will be annexed by the city—perhaps to be offered as prizes in the next Autumn Games. Do I make my meaning plain?"

Carthus's voice was gravel in his throat. "Yes."

"Go then. Your tender in five days, remember.

Send another in."

Carthus left the room as if in a dream, croaked "He wants you now," to the nearest High Council member in the anteroom, and was relieved to find himself outside in the sunlight and the fresh air. Far above him the jeweled heights of the Ponti Bridge stood, as they had stood, glinting and twinkling and shining down on the town, for the last two thousand years.

He squinted: Was it his imagination, or were the jewels less bright, the structure less permanent, the whole glorious bridge subtly less magnificent than before? Was the air of permanence that hung about the bridge beginning to fade away?

Carthus began to calculate the value of the bridge in terms of jewel weight and volume. He wondered how Aathia would treat him if he presented her with the rose diamond from the summit; and the High Council would not view him as a nouveau riche upstart, not him, not if he was the man who bought the Ponti Bridge.

Oh, they would all treat him better. There was no doubt of that.

One by one, the man who called himself Glew

Croll saw the jewel merchants. Each reacted in his or her own way—shock or laughter, sorrow or gloom—at the news of the spell fatigue in the binding of the Ponti Bridge. And, beneath the sneers or the dismay, each of them began to judge profits and balance sheets, mentally judge and guess possible tenders, activate spies in rival jewelers' houses.

Carthus himself told no one anything, not even his beloved, unattainable Aathia. He locked himself in his study and wrote tenders, tore them up, wrote tenders once again. The rest of the jewelers were similarly occupied.

The fire had burned out in the Rogues' Club, leaving only a few red embers in a bed of gray ash, and dawn was painting the sky silver. Gloathis, Redcap, and I had listened to the man called Stoat all night. It was at this point in his narrative that he leaned back on his cushion, and he grinned.

"So there you have it, friends," he said. "A perfect scam. Eh?"

I glanced at Gloathis and Redcap, and was relieved to see that they looked as blank as I felt.

"I'm sorry," said Redcap. "I just don't see . . ."

"You don't see, eh? And what about you, Gloathis? Do you see? Or are your eyes covered with mud?"

Gloathis looked serious. She said, "Well . . . you obviously convinced them all that you were a representative of the Ruling Enclave—and having them all meet in the anteroom was an inspired idea. But I fail to see the profit in this for you. You've said that you need a million, but none of them is going to pay anything to you. They are waiting for a public announcement that will never come, and then the chance to pay their money into the public treasury. . . ."

"You think like a mug," said Stoat. He looked at me and raised an eyebrow. I shook my head. "And you call yourself rogues."

Redcap looked exasperated. "I just don't see the profit in it! You've spent your thirty gold coins on renting the offices and sending the messages. You've told them you're working for the Enclave, and they will pay everything to the Enclave. . . ."

It was hearing Redcap spell it out that did it. I saw it all, and I understood, and as I understood I could feel the laughter welling up inside me. I tried to keep it inside, and the effort almost choked me. "Oh, priceless, priceless," was all I could say for some moments. My friends stared at me, irritated. Stoat said nothing, but he waited.

I got up, leaned in to Stoat, and whispered in his ear. He nodded once, and I began to chortle once again.

"At least one of you has some potential," said Stoat. Then he stood up. He drew his robes around him and swept off down the torch-lined corridors of the Lost Carnadine Rogues' Club, vanishing into the shadows. I stared after him as he left. The other two were looking at me.

"I don't understand," said Redcap.

"What did he do?" begged Gloathis.

"Call yourself rogues?" I asked. "I worked it out for myself. Why can't you two simply . . . Oh, very well. After the jewelers left his office he let them stew for a few days, letting the tension build and build. Then, secretly, he arranged to see each of the jewelers at different times and in different places—probably lowlife taverns.

"And in each tavern he would greet the jeweler and point out the one thing that he—or they—had overlooked. The tenders would be submitted to the Enclave through my friend. He could arrange for the jeweler he was talking to—Carthus, say—to put in the winning tender.

"For of course, he *was* open to bribery."

Gloathis slapped her forehead. "I'm such an oaf! I should have seen it! He could easily have raked in a million gold coins' worth of bribes from that lot. And once the last jeweler paid him, he'd vanish. The jewelers couldn't complain—if the Enclave thought they'd tried to bribe someone they thought to be an Enclave official, they'd be lucky to keep their right arms, let alone their lives and businesses. What a perfect con."

And there was silence in the Hall of the Lost Carnadine Rogues' Club. We were lost in contemplation of the brilliance of the man who sold the Ponti Bridge.

October in the Chair

O CTOBER WAS IN THE chair, so it was chilly that evening, and the leaves were red and orange and tumbled from the trees that circled the grove. The twelve of them sat around a campfire roasting huge sausages on sticks, which spat and crackled as the fat dripped onto the burning applewood, and drinking fresh apple cider, tangy and tart in their mouths.

April took a dainty bite from her sausage, which burst open as she bit into it, spilling hot juice down her chin. "Beshrew and suck ordure on it," she said.

Squat March, sitting next to her, laughed, low and dirty, and then pulled out a huge, filthy handkerchief. "Here you go," he said.

April wiped her chin. "Thanks," she said. "The cursed bag of innards burned me. I'll have a blister there tomorrow."

September yawned. "You are *such* a hypochondriac,"

he said, across the fire. "And such *language*." He had a pencil-thin mustache and was balding in the front, which made his forehead seem high and wise.

"Lay off her," said May. Her dark hair was cropped short against her skull, and she wore sensible boots. She smoked a small brown cigarillo that smelled heavily of cloves. "She's sensitive."

"Oh puh*lease*," said September. "Spare me."

October, conscious of his position in the chair, sipped his apple cider, cleared his throat, and said, "Okay. Who wants to begin?" The chair he sat in was carved from one large block of oakwood, inlaid with ash, with cedar, and with cherrywood. The other eleven sat on tree stumps equally spaced about the small bonfire. The tree stumps had been worn smooth and comfortable by years of use.

"What about the minutes?" asked January. "We always do minutes when I'm in the chair."

"But you aren't in the chair now, are you, dear?" said September, an elegant creature of mock solicitude.

"What about the minutes?" repeated January. "You can't ignore them."

"Let the little buggers take care of themselves," said April, one hand running through her long blonde hair. "And I think September should go first."

September preened and nodded. "Delighted," he said.

"Hey," said February. "Hey-hey-hey-hey-hey-hey-hey. I didn't hear the chairman ratify that. Nobody starts till October says who starts, and then nobody else talks. Can we have maybe the tiniest semblance of order here?" He peered at them, small, pale, dressed entirely in blues and grays.

"It's fine," said October. His beard was all colors, a grove of trees in autumn, deep brown and fire orange and wine red, an untrimmed tangle across the lower half of his face. His cheeks were apple red. He looked like a friend; like someone you had known all your life. "September can go first. Let's just get it rolling."

September placed the end of his sausage into his mouth, chewed daintily, and drained his cider mug. Then he stood up and bowed to the company and began to speak.

"Laurent DeLisle was the finest chef in all of Seattle, at least, Laurent DeLisle thought so, and the Michelin stars on his door confirmed him in his opinion. He was a remarkable chef, it is true—his minced lamb brioche had won several awards; his smoked quail and white truffle ravioli had been described in the *Gastronome* as 'the tenth wonder of the world.' But it was his wine cellar . . . ah, his wine cellar . . . that was his source of pride and his passion.

"I understand that. The last of the white grapes are harvested in me, and the bulk of the reds: I appreciate fine wines, the aroma, the taste, the aftertaste as well.

"Laurent DeLisle bought his wines at auctions, from private wine lovers, from reputable dealers: he would insist on a pedigree for each wine, for wine frauds are, alas, too common, when the bottle is selling for perhaps five, ten, a hundred thousand dollars, or pounds, or euros.

"The treasure—the jewel—the rarest of the rare and the *ne plus ultra* of his temperature-controlled wine cellar was a bottle of 1902 Château Lafitte. It was on the wine list at one hundred and twenty thousand dollars, although it was, in true terms, priceless, for it was the last bottle of its kind."

"Excuse me," said August politely. He was the fattest of them all, his thin hair combed in golden

wisps across his pink pate.

September glared down at his neighbor. "Yes?"

"Is this the one where some rich dude buys the wine to go with the dinner, and the chef decides that the dinner the rich dude ordered isn't good enough for the wine, so he sends out a different dinner, and the guy takes one mouthful, and he's got, like, some rare allergy and he just dies like that, and the wine never gets drunk after all?"

September said nothing. He looked a great deal.

"Because if it is, you told it before. Years ago. Dumb story then. Dumb story now." August smiled. His pink cheeks shone in the firelight.

September said, "Obviously pathos and culture are not to everyone's taste. Some people prefer their barbecues and beer, and some of us like—"

February said, "Well, I hate to say this, but he kind of does have a point. It has to be a new story."

September raised an eyebrow and pursed his lips. "I'm done," he said abruptly. He sat down on his stump.

They looked at one another across the fire, the months of the year.

June, hesitant and clean, raised her hand and said,

"I have one about a guard on the X-ray machines at LaGuardia Airport, who could read all about people from the outlines of their luggage on the screen, and one day she saw a luggage X-ray so beautiful that she fell in love with the person, and she had to figure out which person in the line it was, and she couldn't, and she pined for months and months. And when the person came through again she knew it this time, and it was the man, and he was a wizened old Indian man and she was pretty and black and, like, twenty-five, and she knew it would never work out and she let him go, because she could also see from the shapes of his bags on the screen that he was going to die soon."

October said, "Fair enough, young June. Tell that one."

June stared at him, like a spooked animal. "I just did," she said.

October nodded. "So you did," he said, before any of the others could say anything. And then he said, "Shall we proceed to my story, then?"

February sniffed. "Out of order there, big fella. The man in the chair only tells his story when the rest of us are through. Can't go straight to the main event."

May was placing a dozen chestnuts on the grate above the fire, deploying them into patterns with her tongs. "Let him tell his story if he wants to," she said. "God knows it can't be worse than the one about the wine. And I have things to be getting back to. Flowers don't bloom by themselves. All in favor?"

"You're taking this to a formal vote?" February said. "I cannot believe this. I cannot believe this is happening." He mopped his brow with a handful of tissues, which he pulled from his sleeve.

Seven hands were raised. Four people kept their hands down—February, September, January, and July. ("I don't have anything personal on this," said July apologetically. "It's purely procedural. We shouldn't be setting precedents.")

"It's settled then," said October. "Is there anything anyone would like to say before I begin?"

"Um. Yes. Sometimes," said June, "sometimes I think somebody's watching us from the woods, and then I look and there isn't anybody there. But I still think it."

April said, "That's because you're crazy."

"Mm," said September to everybody. "That's our April. She's sensitive, but she's still the cruelest."

"Enough," said October. He stretched in his chair. He cracked a cobnut with his teeth, pulled out the kernel, and threw the fragments of shell into the fire, where they hissed and spat and popped, and he began.

There was a boy, *October said*, who was miserable at home, although they did not beat him. He did not fit well, not his family, his town, nor even his life. He had two brothers, who were twins, older than he was, and who hurt him or ignored him, and were popular. They played football: some games one twin would score more and be the hero, and some games the other would. Their little brother did not play football. They had a name for their brother. They called him the Runt.

They had called him the Runt since he was a baby, and at first their mother and father had chided them for it.

The twins said, "But he *is* the runt of the litter. Look at *him*. Look at *us*." The boys were six when they said this. Their parents thought it was cute. A name like the Runt can be infectious, so pretty soon the only person who called him Donald was his grandmother, when she telephoned him on his birthday, and people who did not know him.

Now, perhaps because names have power, he was a runt: skinny and small and nervous. He had been born with a runny nose, and it had not stopped running in a decade. At mealtimes, if the twins liked the food, they would steal his; if they did not, they would contrive to place their food on his plate and he would find himself in trouble for leaving good food uneaten.

Their father never missed a football game, and would buy an ice cream afterward for the twin who had scored the most, and a consolation ice cream for the other twin, who hadn't. Their mother described herself as a newspaperwoman, although she mostly sold advertising space and subscriptions: she had gone back to work full-time once the twins were capable of taking care of themselves.

The other kids in the boy's class admired the twins. They had called him Donald for several weeks in first grade, until the word trickled down that his brothers called him the Runt. His teachers rarely called him anything at all, although among themselves they could sometimes be heard to say that it was a pity the youngest Covay boy didn't have the pluck or the imagination or the life of his brothers.

The Runt could not have told you when he first decided to run away, nor when his daydreams crossed the border and became plans. By the time that he admitted to himself he was leaving he had a large Tupperware container hidden beneath a plastic sheet behind the garage containing three Mars bars, two Milky Ways, a bag of nuts, a small bag of licorice, a flashlight, several comics, an unopened packet of beef jerky, and thirty-seven dollars, most of it in quarters. He did not like the taste of beef jerky, but he had read that explorers had survived for weeks on nothing else; and it was when he put the packet of beef jerky into the Tupperware box and pressed the lid down with a pop that he knew he was going to have to run away.

He had read books, newspapers, and magazines. He knew that if you ran away you sometimes met bad people who did bad things to you; but he had also read fairy tales, so he knew that there were kind people out there, side by side with the monsters.

The Runt was a thin ten-year-old, small, with a runny nose and a blank expression. If you were to try and pick him out of a group of boys, you'd be wrong. He'd be the other one. Over at the side. The one your eye slipped over.

All through September he put off leaving. It took a really bad Friday, during the course of which both of his brothers sat on him (and the one who sat on his face broke wind and laughed uproariously), for him to decide that whatever monsters were waiting out in the world would be bearable, perhaps even preferable.

Saturday, his brothers were meant to be looking after him, but soon they went into town to see a girl they liked. The Runt went around the back of the garage and took the Tupperware container out from beneath the plastic sheeting. He took it up to his bedroom. He emptied his schoolbag onto his bed, filled it with his candies and comics and quarters and the beef jerky. He filled an empty soda bottle with water.

The Runt walked into town and got on the bus. He rode west, ten-dollars-in-quarters' worth of west, to a place he didn't know, which he thought was a good start, then he got off the bus and walked. There was no sidewalk now, so when cars came past he would edge over into the ditch, to safety.

The sun was high. He was hungry, so he rummaged in his bag and pulled out a Mars bar. After he ate it he found he was thirsty, and he drank almost half of the water from his soda bottle before he realized he was going to have to ration it. He had thought that once he got out of the town he would see springs of fresh water everywhere, but there were none to be found. There was a river, though, that ran beneath a wide bridge.

The Runt stopped halfway across the bridge to stare down at the brown water. He remembered something he had been told in school: that, in the end, all rivers flowed into the sea. He had never been to the seashore. He clambered down the bank and followed the river. There was a muddy path along the side of the riverbank, and an occasional beer can or plastic snack packet to show that people had been that way before, but he saw no one as he walked.

He finished his water.

He wondered if they were looking for him yet. He imagined police cars and helicopters and dogs, all trying to find him. He would evade them. He would make it to the sea.

The river ran over some rocks, and it splashed. He saw a blue heron, its wings wide, glide past him, and he saw solitary end-of-season dragonflies, and sometimes small clusters of midges, enjoying the Indian summer. The blue sky became dusk gray, and a bat swung down to snatch insects from the air. The Runt wondered where he would sleep that night.

Soon the path divided, and he took the branch that led away from the river, hoping it would lead to a house or to a farm with an empty barn. He walked for some time, as the dusk deepened, until at the end of the path he found a farmhouse, half tumbled down and unpleasant looking. The Runt walked around it, becoming increasingly certain as he walked that nothing could make him go inside, and then he climbed over a broken fence to an abandoned pasture, and settled down to sleep in the long grass with his schoolbag for his pillow.

He lay on his back, fully dressed, staring up at the sky. He was not in the slightest bit sleepy.

"They'll be missing me by now," he told himself. "They'll be worried."

He imagined himself coming home in a few years' time. The delight on his family's faces as he walked up the path to home. Their welcome. Their love. . . .

He woke some hours later, with the bright moonlight in his face. He could see the whole world—as bright as day, like in the nursery rhyme, but pale and without colors. Above him, the moon was full, or almost, and he imagined a face looking down at him, not unkindly, in the shadows and shapes of the moon's surface.

A voice said, "Where do you come from?"

He sat up, not scared, not yet, and looked around him. Trees. Long grass. "Where are you? I don't see you."

Something he had taken for a shadow moved, beside a tree on the edge of the pasture, and he saw a boy of his own age.

"I'm running away from home," said the Runt.

"Whoa," said the boy. "That must have taken a whole lot of guts."

The Runt grinned with pride. He didn't know what to say.

"You want to walk a bit?" said the boy.

"Sure," said the Runt. He moved his schoolbag so it was next to the fence post, so he could always find it again.

They walked down the slope, giving a wide berth to the old farmhouse.

"Does anyone live there?" asked the Runt.

"Not really," said the other boy. He had fair, fine hair that was almost white in the moonlight. "Some people tried a long time back, but they didn't like it, and they left. Then other folk moved in. But nobody lives there now. What's your name?"

"Donald," said the Runt. And then, "But they call me the Runt. What do they call you?"

The boy hesitated. "Dearly," he said.

"That's a cool name."

Dearly said, "I used to have another name, but I can't read it anymore."

They squeezed through a huge iron gateway, rusted part open, part closed, and they were in the little meadow at the bottom of the slope.

"This place is cool," said the Runt.

There were dozens of stones of all sizes in the small meadow. Tall stones, bigger than either of the boys, and small ones, just the right size for sitting on. There were some broken stones. The Runt knew what sort of a place this was, but it did not scare him. It was a loved place.

"Who's buried here?" he asked.

"Mostly okay people," said Dearly. "There used to be a town over there. Past those trees. Then the rail-road came and they built a stop in the next town over, and our town sort of dried up and fell in and blew away. There's bushes and trees now, where the town was. You can hide in the trees and go into the old houses and jump out."

The Runt said, "Are they like that farmhouse up there? The houses?" He didn't want to go in them, if they were.

"No," said Dearly. "Nobody goes in them, except for me. And some animals, sometimes. I'm the only kid around here."

"I figured," said the Runt.

"Maybe we can go down and play in them," said Dearly.

"That would be pretty cool," said the Runt.

It was a perfect early October night: almost as warm as summer, and the harvest moon dominated the sky. You could see everything.

"Which one of these is yours?" asked the Runt.

Dearly straightened up proudly and took the Runt by the hand. He pulled him to an overgrown corner of the field. The two boys pushed aside the long grass. The stone was set flat into the ground, and it had dates carved into it from a hundred years before. Much of it was worn away, but beneath the dates it was possible to make out the words

DEARLY DEPARTED

WILL NEVER BE FORG

"Forgotten, I'd wager," said Dearly.

"Yeah, that's what I'd say too," said the Runt.

They went out of the gate, down a gully, and into what remained of the old town. Trees grew through houses, and buildings had fallen in on themselves, but it wasn't scary. They played hide-and-seek. They explored. Dearly showed the Runt some pretty cool places, including a one-room cottage that he said was the oldest building in that whole part of the county. It was in pretty good shape, too, considering how old it was.

"I can see pretty good by moonlight," said the Runt. "Even inside. I didn't know that it was so easy."

"Yeah," said Dearly. "And after a while you get good at seeing even when there ain't any moonlight."

The Runt was envious.

"I got to go to the bathroom," said the Runt. "Is there somewhere around here?"

Dearly thought for a moment. "I don't know," he admitted. "I don't do that stuff anymore. There are a few outhouses still standing, but they may not be safe. Best just to do it in the woods."

"Like a bear," said the Runt.

He walked out the back, into the woods that pushed up against the wall of the cottage, and went behind a tree. He'd never done that before, in the open air. He felt like a wild animal. When he was done he wiped himself off with fallen leaves. Then he went back out the front. Dearly was sitting in a pool of moonlight, waiting for him.

"How did you die?" asked the Runt.

"I got sick," said Dearly. "My maw cried and carried on something fierce. Then I died."

"If I stayed here with you," said the Runt, "would I have to be dead, too?"

"Maybe," said Dearly. "Well, yeah. I guess."

"What's it like? Being dead?"

"I don't mind it," admitted Dearly. "Worst thing is not having anyone to play with."

"But there must be lots of people up in that

meadow," said the Runt. "Don't they ever play with you?"

"Nope," said Dearly. "Mostly, they sleep. And even when they walk, they can't be bothered to just go and see stuff and do things. They can't be bothered with me. You see that tree?"

It was a beech tree, its smooth gray bark cracked with age. It sat in what must once have been the town square, ninety years before.

"Yeah," said the Runt.

"You want to climb it?"

"It looks kind of high."

"It is. Real high. But it's easy to climb. I'll show you."

It was easy to climb. There were handholds in the bark, and the boys went up the big beech like a couple of monkeys or pirates or warriors. From the top of the tree one could see the whole world. The sky was starting to lighten, just a hair, in the east.

Everything waited. The night was ending. The world was holding its breath, preparing to begin again.

"This was the best day I ever had," said the Runt.

"Me too," said Dearly. "What you going to do now?"

"I don't know," said the Runt.

He imagined himself going on across the world, all the way to the sea. He imagined himself growing up and growing older, bringing himself up by his bootstraps. Somewhere in there he would become fabulously wealthy. And then he would go back to the house with the twins in it, and he would drive up to their door in his wonderful car, or perhaps he would turn up at a football game (in his imagination the twins had neither aged nor grown) and look down at them in a kindly way. He would buy them all—the twins, his parents—a meal at the finest restaurant in the city, and they would tell him how badly they had misunderstood him and mistreated him. They apologized and wept, and through it all he said nothing. He let their apologies wash over him. And then he would give each of them a gift, and afterward he would leave their lives once more, this time for good.

It was a fine dream.

In reality, he knew, he would keep walking, and be found tomorrow or the day after that, and go home and be yelled at, and everything would be the same as it ever was, and day after day, hour after hour until the end of time he'd still be the Runt, only now they'd be mad at him for having dared to walk away.

"I have to go to bed soon," said Dearly. He started to climb down the big beech tree.

Climbing down the tree was harder, the Runt found. You couldn't see where you were putting your feet and had to feel around for somewhere to put them. Several times he slipped and slid, but Dearly went down ahead of him and would say things like "A little to the right, now," and they both made it down just fine.

The sky continued to lighten, and the moon was fading, and it was harder to see. They clambered back through the gully. Sometimes the Runt wasn't sure that Dearly was there at all, but when he got to the top, he saw the boy waiting for him.

They didn't say much as they walked up to the meadow filled with stones. The Runt put his arm over Dearly's shoulder, and they walked in step up the hill.

"Well," said Dearly. "Thanks for coming over."

"I had a good time," said the Runt.

"Yeah," said Dearly. "Me too."

Down in the woods somewhere a bird began to sing.

"If I wanted to stay—?" said the Runt, all in a

burst. Then he stopped. *I might never get another chance to change it*, thought the Runt. He'd never get to the sea. They'd never let him.

Dearly didn't say anything, not for a long time. The world was gray. More birds joined the first.

"I can't do it," said Dearly eventually. "But they might."

"Who?"

"The ones in there." The fair boy pointed up the slope to the tumbledown farmhouse with the jagged, broken windows, silhouetted against the dawn. The gray light had not changed it.

The Runt shivered. "There's people in there?" he said. "I thought you said it was empty."

"It ain't empty," said Dearly. "I said nobody lives there. Different things." He looked up at the sky. "I got to go now," he added. He squeezed the Runt's hand. And then he just wasn't there any longer.

The Runt stood in the little graveyard all on his own, listening to the birdsong on the morning air. Then he made his way up the hill. It was harder by himself.

He picked up his schoolbag from the place he had left it. He ate his last Milky Way and stared at the tumbledown building. The empty windows of the farmhouse were like eyes, watching him.

It was darker inside there. Darker than anything.

He pushed his way through the weed-choked yard. The door to the farmhouse was mostly crumbled away. He stopped at the doorway, hesitating, wondering if this was wise. He could smell damp, and rot, and something else underneath. He thought he heard something move, deep in the house, in the cellar, maybe, or the attic. A shuffle, maybe. Or a hop. It was hard to tell.

Eventually, he went inside.

Nobody said anything. October filled his wooden mug with apple cider when he was done, and drained it, and filled it again.

"It was a story," said December. "I'll say that for it." He rubbed his pale blue eyes with a fist. The fire was almost out.

"What happened next?" asked June nervously. "After he went into the house?"

May, sitting next to her, put her hand on June's arm. "Better not to think about it," she said.

"Anyone else want a turn?" asked August. There

was silence. "Then I think we're done."

"That needs to be an official motion," pointed out February.

"All in favor?" said October. There was a chorus of "ayes." "All against?" Silence. "Then I declare this meeting adjourned."

They got up from the fireside, stretching and yawning, and walked away into the wood, in ones and twos and threes, until only October and his neighbor remained.

"Your turn in the chair next time," said October.

"I know," said November. He was pale and thin lipped. He helped October out of the wooden chair. "I like your stories. Mine are always too dark."

"I don't think so," said October. "It's just that your nights are longer. And you aren't as warm."

"Put it like that," said November, "and I feel better. I suppose we can't help who we are."

"That's the spirit," said his brother. And they touched hands as they walked away from the fire's orange embers, taking their stories with them back into the dark.

For Ray Bradbury

Chivalry

MRS. WHITAKER FOUND THE Holy Grail; it was under a fur coat.

Every Thursday afternoon Mrs. Whitaker walked down to the post office to collect her pension, even though her legs were no longer what they were, and on the way back home she would stop in at the Oxfam Shop and buy herself a little something.

The Oxfam Shop sold old clothes, knickknacks, oddments, bits and bobs, and large quantities of old paperbacks, all of them donations: secondhand flotsam, often the house clearances of the dead. All the profits went to charity.

The shop was staffed by volunteers. The volunteer on duty this afternoon was Marie, seventeen, slightly overweight, and dressed in a baggy mauve jumper which looked like she had bought it from the shop.

Marie sat by the till with a copy of *Modern*

Woman magazine, filling out a "Reveal Your Hidden Personality" questionnaire. Every now and then, she'd flip to the back of the magazine and check the relative points assigned to an A), B), or C) answer before making up her mind how she'd respond to the question.

Mrs. Whitaker puttered around the shop.

They still hadn't sold the stuffed cobra, she noted. It had been there for six months now, gathering dust, glass eyes gazing balefully at the clothes racks and the cabinet filled with chipped porcelain and chewed toys.

Mrs. Whitaker patted its head as she went past.

She picked out a couple of Mills & Boon novels from a bookshelf—*Her Thundering Soul* and *Her Turbulent Heart*, a shilling each—and gave careful consideration to the empty bottle of Mateus Rosé with a decorative lampshade on it before deciding she really didn't have anywhere to put it.

She moved a rather threadbare fur coat, which smelled badly of mothballs. Underneath it was a walking stick and a water-stained copy of *Romance and Legend of Chivalry* by A. R. Hope Moncrieff, priced at five pence. Next to the book, on its side, was the Holy Grail. It had a little round paper sticker on the base, and written on it, in felt pen, was the price: 30p.

Mrs. Whitaker picked up the dusty silver goblet and appraised it through her thick spectacles.

"This is nice," she called to Marie.

Marie shrugged.

"It'd look nice on the mantelpiece."

Marie shrugged again.

Mrs. Whitaker gave fifty pence to Marie, who gave her ten pence change and a brown paper bag to put the books and the Holy Grail in. Then she went next door to the butcher's and bought herself a nice piece of liver. Then she went home.

The inside of the goblet was thickly coated with a brownish-red dust. Mrs. Whitaker washed it out with great care, then left it to soak for an hour in warm water with a dash of vinegar added.

Then she polished it with metal polish until it gleamed, and she put it on the mantelpiece in her parlor, where it sat between a small soulful china basset hound and a photograph of her late husband, Henry, on the beach at Frinton in 1953.

She had been right: It did look nice.

For dinner that evening she had the liver fried in breadcrumbs with onions. It was very nice.

The next morning was Friday; on alternate Fridays Mrs. Whitaker and Mrs. Greenberg would visit each other. Today it was Mrs. Greenberg's turn to visit Mrs. Whitaker. They sat in the parlor and ate macaroons and drank tea. Mrs. Whitaker took one sugar in her tea, but Mrs. Greenberg took sweetener, which she always carried in her handbag in a small plastic container.

"That's nice," said Mrs. Greenberg, pointing to the Grail. "What is it?"

"It's the Holy Grail," said Mrs. Whitaker. "It's the cup that Jesus drunk out of at the Last Supper. Later, at the Crucifixion, it caught His precious blood when the centurion's spear pierced His side."

Mrs. Greenberg sniffed. She was small and Jewish and didn't hold with unsanitary things. "I wouldn't know about that," she said, "but it's very nice. Our Myron got one just like that when he won the swimming tournament, only it's got his name on the side."

"Is he still with that nice girl? The hairdresser?"

"Bernice? Oh yes. They're thinking of getting engaged," said Mrs. Greenberg.

"That's nice," said Mrs. Whitaker. She took another macaroon.

Mrs. Greenberg baked her own macaroons and brought them over every alternate Friday: small sweet light-brown biscuits with almonds on top.

They talked about Myron and Bernice, and Mrs. Whitaker's nephew Ronald (she had had no children), and about their friend Mrs. Perkins who was in hospital with her hip, poor dear.

At midday Mrs. Greenberg went home, and Mrs. Whitaker made herself cheese on toast for lunch, and after lunch Mrs. Whitaker took her pills: the white and the red and two little orange ones.

The doorbell rang.

Mrs. Whitaker answered the door. It was a young man with shoulder-length hair so fair it was almost white, wearing gleaming silver armor, with a white surcoat.

"Hello," he said.

"Hello," said Mrs. Whitaker.

"I'm on a quest," he said.

"That's nice," said Mrs. Whitaker noncommitally.

"Can I come in?" he asked.

Mrs. Whitaker shook her head. "I'm sorry, I don't

think so," she said.

"I'm on a quest for the Holy Grail," the young man said. "Is it here?"

"Have you got any identification?" Mrs. Whitaker asked. She knew that it was unwise to let unidentified strangers into your home when you were elderly and living on your own. Handbags get emptied, and worse than that.

The young man went back down the garden path. His horse, a huge gray charger, big as a shire horse, its head high and its eyes intelligent, was tethered to Mrs. Whitaker's garden gate. The knight fumbled in the saddlebag and returned with a scroll.

It was signed by Arthur, King of All Britons, and charged all persons of whatever rank or station to know that here was Galaad, Knight of the Table Round, and that he was on a Right High and Noble Quest. There was a drawing of the young man below that. It wasn't a bad likeness.

Mrs. Whitaker nodded. She had been expecting a little card with a photograph on it, but this was far more impressive.

"I suppose you had better come in," she said.

They went into her kitchen. She made Galaad a

cup of tea, then she took him into the parlor.

Galaad saw the Grail on her mantelpiece, and dropped to one knee. He put down the teacup carefully on the russet carpet. A shaft of light came through the net curtains and painted his awed face with golden sunlight and turned his hair into a silver halo.

"It is truly the Sangrail," he said very quietly. He blinked his pale blue eyes three times, very fast, as if he were blinking back tears.

He lowered his head as if in silent prayer.

Galaad stood up again and turned to Mrs. Whitaker. "Gracious lady, keeper of the Holy of Holies, let me now depart this place with the Blessed Chalice, that my journeyings may be ended and my geas fulfilled."

"Sorry?" said Mrs. Whitaker.

Galaad walked over to her and took her old hands in his. "My quest is over," he told her. "The Sangrail is finally within my reach."

Mrs. Whitaker pursed her lips. "Can you pick your teacup and saucer up, please?" she said.

Galaad picked up his teacup apologetically.

"No. I don't think so," said Mrs. Whitaker. "I rather

like it there. It's just right, between the dog and the photograph of my Henry."

"Is it gold you need? Is that it? Lady, I can bring you gold. . . ."

"No," said Mrs. Whitaker. "I don't want any gold, thank *you*. I'm simply not interested."

She ushered Galaad to the front door. "Nice to meet you," she said.

His horse was leaning its head over her garden fence, nibbling her gladioli. Several of the neighborhood children were standing on the pavement, watching it.

Galaad took some sugar lumps from the saddlebag, and showed the braver of the children how to feed the horse, their hands held flat. The children giggled. One of the older girls stroked the horse's nose.

Galaad swung himself up onto the horse in one fluid movement. Then the horse and the knight trotted off down Hawthorne Crescent.

Mrs. Whitaker watched them until they were out of sight, then sighed and went back inside.

The weekend was quiet.

On Saturday Mrs. Whitaker took the bus into

Maresfield to visit her nephew Ronald, his wife, Euphonia, and their daughters, Clarissa and Dillian. She took them a currant cake she had baked herself.

On Sunday morning Mrs. Whitaker went to church. Her local church was St. James the Less, which was a little more "Don't think of this as a church, think of it as a place where like-minded friends hang out and are joyful" than Mrs. Whitaker felt entirely comfortable with, but she liked the vicar, the Reverend Bartholomew, when he wasn't actually playing the guitar.

After the service, she thought about mentioning to him that she had the Holy Grail in her front parlor, but decided against it.

On Monday morning Mrs. Whitaker was working in the back garden. She had a small herb garden she was extremely proud of: dill, vervain, mint, rosemary, thyme, and a wild expanse of parsley. She was down on her knees, wearing thick green gardening gloves, weeding, and picking out slugs and putting them in a plastic bag.

Mrs. Whitaker was very tenderhearted when it came to slugs. She would take them down to the back of her garden, which bordered on the railway line, and throw them over the fence.

She cut some parsley for the salad. There was a cough behind her. Galaad stood there, tall and beautiful, his armor glinting in the morning sun. In his arms he held a long package, wrapped in oiled leather.

"I'm back," he said.

"Hello," said Mrs. Whitaker. She stood up, rather slowly, and took off her gardening gloves. "Well," she said, "now you're here, you might as well make yourself useful."

She gave him the plastic bag full of slugs and told him to tip the slugs out over the back of the fence.

He did.

Then they went into the kitchen.

"Tea? Or lemonade?" she asked.

"Whatever you're having," Galaad said.

Mrs. Whitaker took a jug of her homemade lemonade from the fridge and sent Galaad outside to pick a sprig of mint. She selected two tall glasses. She washed the mint carefully and put a few leaves in each glass, then poured the lemonade.

"Is your horse outside?" she asked.

"Oh yes. His name is Grizzel."

"And you've come a long way, I suppose."

"A very long way."

"I see," said Mrs. Whitaker. She took a blue plastic basin from under the sink and half filled it with water. Galaad took it out to Grizzel. He waited while the horse drank and brought the empty basin back to Mrs. Whitaker.

"Now," she said, "I suppose you're still after the Grail."

"Aye, still do I seek the Sangrail," he said. He picked up the leather package from the floor, put it down on her tablecloth, and unwrapped it. "For it, I offer you this."

It was a sword, its blade almost four feet long. There were words and symbols traced elegantly along the length of the blade. The hilt was worked in silver and gold, and a large jewel was set in the pommel.

"It's very nice," said Mrs. Whitaker doubtfully.

"This," said Galaad, "is the sword Balmung, forged by Wayland Smith in the dawn times. Its twin is Flamberge. Who wears it is unconquerable in war, and invincible in battle. Who wears it is incapable of a cowardly act or an ignoble one. Set in its pommel is the sardonyx Bircone, which protects its possessor from poison slipped into wine or ale, and from the treachery of friends."

Mrs. Whitaker peered at the sword. "It must be very sharp," she said, after a while.

"It can slice a falling hair in twain. Nay, it could slice a sunbeam," said Galaad, proudly.

"Well, then, maybe you ought to put it away," said Mrs. Whitaker.

"Don't you want it?" Galaad seemed disappointed.

"No, thank you," said Mrs. Whitaker. It occurred to her that her late husband, Henry, would have quite liked it. He would have hung it on the wall in his study next to the stuffed carp he had caught in Scotland, and pointed it out to visitors.

Galaad rewrapped the oiled leather around the sword Balmung and tied it up with white cord.

He sat there, disconsolate.

Mrs. Whitaker made him some cream cheese and cucumber sandwiches for the journey back and wrapped them in greaseproof paper. She gave him an apple for Grizell. He seemed very pleased with both gifts.

She waved them both good-bye.

That afternoon she took the bus down to the hospital to see Mrs. Perkins, who was still in with her hip, poor love. Mrs. Whitaker took her some homemade fruitcake, although she had left out the walnuts from the recipe, because Mrs. Perkins's teeth weren't what they used to be.

She watched a little television that evening, and had an early night.

On Tuesday the postman called. Mrs. Whitaker was up in the boxroom at the top of the house, doing a spot of tidying, and, taking each step slowly and carefully, she didn't make it downstairs in time. The postman had left her a message which said that he'd tried to deliver a packet, but no one was home.

Mrs. Whitaker sighed.

She put the message into her handbag and went down to the post office.

The package was from her niece Shirelle in Sydney, Australia. It contained photographs of her husband, Wallace, and her two daughters, Dixie and Violet, and a conch shell packed in cotton wool.

Mrs. Whitaker had a number of ornamental shells in her bedroom. Her favorite had a view of the

Bahamas done on it in enamel. It had been a gift from her sister, Ethel, who had died in 1983.

She put the shell and the photographs in her shopping bag. Then, seeing that she was in the area, she stopped in at the Oxfam Shop on her way home.

"Hullo Mrs. W.," said Marie.

Mrs. Whitaker stared at her. Marie was wearing lipstick (possibly not the best shade for her, nor particularly expertly applied, but, thought Mrs. Whitaker, that would come with time) and a rather smart skirt. It was a great improvement.

"Oh. Hello, dear," said Mrs. Whitaker.

"There was a man in here last week, asking about that thing you bought. The little metal cup thing. I told him where to find you. You don't mind, do you?"

"No, dear," said Mrs. Whitaker. "He found me."

"He was really dreamy. Really, really dreamy," sighed Marie wistfully. "I could of gone for him.

"And he had a big white horse and all," Marie concluded. She was standing up straighter as well, Mrs. Whitaker noted approvingly.

On the bookshelf Mrs. Whitaker found a new Mills & Boon novel—*Her Majestic Passion*—

although she hadn't yet finished the two she had bought on her last visit.

She picked up the copy of *Romance and Legend of Chivalry* and opened it. It smelled musty. EX LIBRIS FISHER was neatly handwritten at the top of the first page in red ink.

She put it down where she had found it.

When she got home, Galaad was waiting for her. He was giving the neighborhood children rides on Grizell's back, up and down the street.

"I'm glad you're here," she said. "I've got some cases that need moving."

She showed him up to the boxroom in the top of the house. He moved all the old suitcases for her, so she could get to the cupboard at the back.

It was very dusty up there.

She kept him up there most of the afternoon, moving things around while she dusted.

Galaad had a cut on his cheek, and he held one arm a little stiffly.

They talked a little while she dusted and tidied. Mrs. Whitaker told him about her late husband, Henry; and how the life insurance had paid the house off; and how she had all these things, but no one really to leave them to, no one but Ronald really, and his wife only liked modern things. She told him how she had met Henry during the war, when he was in the ARP and she hadn't closed the kitchen blackout curtains all the way; and about the sixpenny dances they went to in the town; and how they'd gone to London when the war had ended, and she'd had her first drink of wine.

Galaad told Mrs. Whitaker about his mother, Elaine, who was flighty and no better than she should have been and something of a witch to boot; and his grandfather King Pelles, who was well-meaning although at best a little vague; and of his youth in the Castle of Bliant on the Joyous Isle; and his father, whom he knew as "Le Chevalier Mal Fet," who was more or less completely mad, and was in reality Lancelot du Lac, greatest of knights, in disguise and bereft of his wits; and of Galaad's days as a young squire in Camelot.

At five o'clock Mrs. Whitaker surveyed the box-room and decided that it met with her approval; then she opened the window so the room could air, and they went downstairs to the kitchen, where she put on the kettle.

Galaad sat down at the kitchen table.

He opened the leather purse at his waist and took out a round white stone. It was about the size of a cricket ball.

"My lady," he said, "this is for you, an you give me the Sangrail."

Mrs. Whitaker picked up the stone, which was heavier than it looked, and held it up to the light. It was milkily translucent, and deep inside it flecks of silver glittered and glinted in the late-afternoon sunlight. It was warm to the touch.

Then, as she held it, a strange feeling crept over her: Deep inside she felt stillness and a sort of peace. *Serenity*, that was the word for it; she felt serene.

Reluctantly she put the stone back on the table.

"It's very nice," she said.

"That is the Philosopher's Stone, which our forefather Noah hung in the Ark to give light when there was no light; it can transform base metals into gold; and it has certain other properties," Galaad told her proudly. "And that isn't all. There's more. Here." From the leather bag he took an egg and handed it to her.

It was the size of a goose egg and was a shiny

black, mottled with scarlet and white. When Mrs. Whitaker touched it, the hairs on the back of her neck prickled. Her immediate impression was one of incredible heat and freedom. She heard the crackling of distant fires, and for a fraction of a second she seemed to feel herself far above the world, swooping and diving on wings of flame.

She put the egg down on the table, next to the Philosopher's Stone.

"That is the Egg of the Phoenix," said Galaad. "From far Araby it comes. One day it will hatch out into the Phoenix bird itself; and when its time comes, the bird will build a nest of flame, lay its egg, and die, to be reborn in flame in a later age of the world."

"I thought that was what it was," said Mrs. Whitaker.

"And, last of all, lady," said Galaad, "I have brought you this."

He drew it from his pouch, and gave it to her. It was an apple, apparently carved from a single ruby, on an amber stem.

A little nervously, she picked it up. It was soft to the touch—deceptively so: Her fingers bruised it, and ruby-colored juice from the apple ran down Mrs. Whitaker's hand.

The kitchen filled—almost imperceptibly, magically—with the smell of summer fruit, of raspberries and peaches and strawberries and red currants. As if from a great way away she heard distant voices raised in song and far music on the air.

"It is one of the apples of the Hesperides," said Galaad quietly. "One bite from it will heal any illness or wound, no matter how deep; a second bite restores youth and beauty; and a third bite is said to grant eternal life."

Mrs. Whitaker licked the sticky juice from her hand. It tasted like fine wine.

There was a moment, then, when it all came back to her—how it was to be young: to have a firm, slim body that would do whatever she wanted it to do; to run down a country lane for the simple unladylike joy of running; to have men smile at her just because she was herself and happy about it.

Mrs. Whitaker looked at Sir Galaad, most comely of all knights, sitting fair and noble in her small kitchen.

She caught her breath.

"And that's all I have brought for you," said Galaad. "They weren't easy to get, either."

Mrs. Whitaker put the ruby fruit down on her kitchen table. She looked at the Philosopher's Stone, and the Egg of the Phoenix, and the Apple of Life.

Then she walked into her parlor and looked at the mantelpiece: at the little china basset hound, and the Holy Grail, and the photograph of her late husband, Henry, shirtless, smiling and eating an ice cream in black and white almost forty years away.

She went back into the kitchen. The kettle had begun to whistle. She poured a little steaming water into the teapot, swirled it around, and poured it out. Then she added two spoonfuls of tea and one for the pot and poured in the rest of the water. All this she did in silence.

She turned to Galaad then, and she looked at him.

"Put that apple away," she told Galaad firmly. "You shouldn't offer things like that to old ladies. It isn't proper."

She paused, then. "But I'll take the other two," she continued, after a moment's thought. "They'll look nice on the mantelpiece. And two for one's fair, or I don't know what is."

Galaad beamed. He put the ruby apple into his leather pouch. Then he went down on one knee, and kissed Mrs. Whitaker's hand.

"Stop that," said Mrs. Whitaker. She poured them both cups of tea, after getting out the very best china, which was only for special occasions.

They sat in silence, drinking their tea.

When they had finished their tea they went into the parlor.

Galaad crossed himself, and picked up the Grail.

Mrs. Whitaker arranged the Egg and the Stone where the Grail had been. The Egg kept tipping on one side, and she propped it up against the little china dog.

"They do look very nice," said Mrs. Whitaker.

"Yes," agreed Galaad. "They look very nice."

"Can I give you anything to eat before you go back?" she asked.

He shook his head.

"Some fruitcake," she said. "You may not think you want any now, but you'll be glad of it in a few hours' time. And you should probably use the facilities. Now, give me that, and I'll wrap it up for you."

She directed him to the small toilet at the end of

the hall, and went into the kitchen, holding the Grail. She had some old Christmas wrapping paper in the pantry, and she wrapped the Grail in it, and tied the package with twine. Then she cut a large slice of fruitcake and put it in a brown paper bag, along with a banana and a slice of processed cheese in silver foil.

Galaad came back from the toilet. She gave him the paper bag, and the Holy Grail. Then she went up on tiptoes and kissed him on the cheek.

"You're a nice boy," she said. "You take care of yourself."

He hugged her, and she shooed him out of the kitchen, and out of the back door, and she shut the door behind him. She poured herself another cup of tea, and cried quietly into a Kleenex, while the sound of hoofbeats echoed down Hawthorne Crescent.

On Wednesday Mrs. Whitaker stayed in all day.

On Thursday she went down the post office to collect her pension. Then she stopped in at the Oxfam Shop.

The woman on the till was new to her. "Where's Marie?" asked Mrs. Whitaker.

The woman on the till, who had blue-rinsed gray hair and blue spectacles that went up into diamanté points, shook her head and shrugged her shoulders. "She went off with a young man," she said. "On a horse. *Tch*. I ask you. I'm meant to be down in the Heathfield shop this afternoon. I had to get my Johnny to run me up here, while we find someone else."

"Oh," said Mrs. Whitaker. "Well, it's nice that she's found herself a young man."

"Nice for her, maybe," said the lady on the till, "but some of us were meant to be in Heathfield this afternoon."

On a shelf near the back of the shop Mrs. Whitaker found a tarnished old silver container with a long spout. It had been priced at sixty pence, according to the little paper label stuck to the side. It looked a little like a flattened, elongated teapot.

She picked out a Mills & Boon novel she hadn't read before. It was called *Her Singular Love*. She took the book and the silver container up to the woman on the till.

"Sixty-five pee, dear," said the woman, picking up the silver object, staring at it. "Funny old thing, isn't it? Came in this morning." It had writing carved along the side in blocky old Chinese characters and an elegant arching handle. "Some kind of oil can, I suppose."

"No, it's not an oil can," said Mrs. Whitaker, who knew exactly what it was. "It's a lamp."

There was a small metal finger ring, unornamented, tied to the handle of the lamp with brown twine.

"Actually," said Mrs. Whitaker, "on second thoughts, I think I'll just have the book."

She paid her five pence for the novel, and put the lamp back where she had found it, in the back of the shop. After all, Mrs. Whitaker reflected, as she walked home, it wasn't as if she had anywhere to put it.

The Price

TRAMPS AND VAGABONDS HAVE marks they make on gateposts and trees and doors, letting others of their kind know a little about the people who live at the houses and farms they pass on their travels. I think cats must leave similar signs; how else to explain the cats who turn up at our door through the year, hungry and flea-ridden and abandoned?

We take them in. We get rid of the fleas and the ticks, feed them, and take them to the vet. We pay for them to get their shots, and, indignity upon indignity, we have them neutered or spayed.

And they stay with us, for a few months, or for a year, or forever.

Most of them arrive in summer. We live in the country, just the right distance out of town for the city dwellers to abandon their cats near us.

We never seem to have more than eight cats, rarely have less than three. The cat population of my house is currently as follows: Hermione and Pod, tabby and black respectively, the mad sisters who live in my attic office and do not mingle; Snowflake, the blue-eyed long-haired white cat, who lived wild in the woods for years before she gave up her wild ways for soft sofas and beds; and, last but largest, Furball, Snowflake's cushionlike calico long-haired daughter, orange and black and white, whom I discovered as a tiny kitten in our garage one day, strangled and almost dead, her head poked through an old badminton net, and who surprised us all by not dying but instead growing up to be the best-natured cat I have ever encountered.

And then there is the black cat. Who has no other name than the Black Cat and who turned up almost a month ago. We did not realize he was going to be living here at first: he looked too well fed to be a stray, too old and jaunty to have been abandoned. He looked like a small panther, and he moved like a patch of night.

One day, in the summer, he was lurking about our ramshackle porch: eight or nine years old, at a guess, male, greenish-yellow of eye, very friendly, quite unperturbable. I assumed he belonged to a

neighboring farmer or household.

I went away for a few weeks, to finish writing a book, and when I came home he was still on our porch, living in an old cat bed one of the children had found for him. He was, however, almost unrecognizable. Patches of fur had gone, and there were deep scratches on his gray skin. The tip of one ear was chewed away. There was a gash beneath one eye, a slice gone from one lip. He looked tired and thin.

We took the Black Cat to the vet, where we got him some antibiotics, which we fed him each night, along with soft cat food.

We wondered who he was fighting. Snowflake, our beautiful white near-feral queen? Raccoons? A rat-tailed, fanged possum?

Each night the scratches would be worse—one night his side would be chewed up; the next it would be his underbelly, raked with claw marks and bloody to the touch.

When it got to that point, I took him down to the basement to recover beside the furnace and the piles of boxes. He was surprisingly heavy, the Black Cat, and I picked him up and carried him down there, with a cat basket, and a litter box, and some food and water. I closed the door behind me. I had to wash the blood from my hands when I left the basement.

He stayed down there for four days. At first he seemed too weak to feed himself: a cut beneath one eye had rendered him almost one-eyed, and he limped and lolled weakly, thick yellow pus oozing from the cut in his lip.

I went down there every morning and every night, and I fed him and gave him antibiotics, which I mixed with his canned food, and I dabbed at the worst of the cuts, and spoke to him. He had diarrhea, and, although I changed his litter daily, the basement stank evilly.

The four days that the Black Cat lived in the basement were a bad four days in my house: the baby slipped in the bath and banged her head and might have drowned; I learned that a project I had set my heart on—adapting Hope Mirrlees's novel *Lud-in-the-Mist* for the BBC—was no longer going to happen, and I realized that I did not have the energy to begin again from scratch, pitching it to other networks or to other media; my daughter left for summer camp and immediately began to send home a plethora of heart-tearing letters and cards, five or six each day, imploring us to bring her home; my son had some kind of fight with his best friend, to the point that they were no longer on speaking terms; and, returning home one night, my wife hit a deer that ran out in front of the car. The deer was killed, the car was left undriveable, and my wife sustained a small cut over one eye.

By the fourth day, the cat was prowling the basement, walking haltingly but impatiently between the stacks of books and comics, the boxes of mail and cassettes, of pictures and of gifts and of stuff. He mewed at me to let him out and, reluctantly, I did so.

He went back onto the porch and slept there for the rest of the day.

The next morning there were deep, new gashes in his flanks, and clumps of black cat hair—his—covered the wooden boards of the porch.

Letters arrived that day from my daughter, telling us that camp was going better and she thought she could survive a few days; my son and his friend sorted out their problem, although what the argument was about—trading cards, computer games, *Star Wars*, or A Girl—I would never learn. The BBC executive who had vetoed *Lud-in-the-Mist* was discovered to have been taking bribes (well, "questionable loans") from an independent production company and was sent home on permanent leave: his successor, I was delighted to learn when she faxed me, was the woman who had initially proposed the project to me before leaving the BBC.

I thought about returning the Black Cat to the basement, but decided against it. Instead, I resolved to try and discover what kind of animal was coming to our house each night and from there to formulate a plan of action—to trap it, perhaps.

For birthdays and at Christmas my family gives me gadgets and gizmos, pricy toys which excite my fancy but, ultimately, rarely leave their boxes. There is a food dehydrator and an electric carving knife, a bread-making machine, and, last year's present, a pair of see-in-the-dark binoculars. On Christmas Day I had put the batteries into the binoculars and had walked about the basement in the dark, too impatient even to wait until nightfall, stalking a flock of imaginary Starlings. (You were warned not to turn it on in the light: that would have damaged the binoculars and quite possibly your eyes as well.) Afterward I had put the device back into its box, and it sat there still, in my office, beside the box of computer cables and forgotten bits and pieces.

Perhaps, I thought, if the creature—dog or cat or raccoon or what have you—were to see me sitting on the porch, it would not come, so I took a chair into the box and coatroom, little larger than a closet, which overlooks the porch, and, when everyone in the house was asleep, I went out onto the porch and bade the Black Cat good night.

That cat, my wife had said, when he first arrived, *is a person.* And there was something very person-like in his huge leonine face: his broad black nose, his greenish-yellow eyes, his fanged but amiable mouth (still leaking amber pus from the right lower lip).

I stroked his head, and scratched him beneath the chin, and wished him well. Then I went inside and turned off the light on the porch.

I sat on my chair, in the darkness inside the house with the see-in-the-dark binoculars on my lap. I had switched the binoculars on, and a trickle of greenish light came from the eyepieces.

Time passed, in the darkness.

I experimented with looking at the darkness with the binoculars, learning to focus, to see the world in shades of green. I found myself horrified by the number of swarming insects I could see in the night air: it was as if the night world were some kind of nightmarish soup, swimming with life. Then I lowered the binoculars from my eyes and stared out at the rich blacks and blues of the night, empty and peaceful and calm.

Time passed. I struggled to keep awake, found myself profoundly missing cigarettes and coffee, my two lost addictions. Either of them would have kept my eyes open. But before I had tumbled too far into the world of sleep and dreams, a yowl from the garden jerked me fully awake. I fumbled the binoculars to my eyes, and was disappointed to see that it was merely Snowflake, the white cat, streaking across the front garden like a patch of greenish-white light. She vanished into the woodland to the left of the house and was gone.

I was about to settle myself back down when it occurred to me to wonder what exactly had startled

Snowflake so, and I began scanning the middle distance with the binoculars, looking for a huge raccoon, a dog, or a vicious possum. And there was indeed something coming down the driveway toward the house. I could see it through the binoculars, clear as day.

It was the Devil.

I had never seen the Devil before, and, although I had written about him in the past, if pressed would have confessed that I had no belief in him, other than as an imaginary figure, tragic and Miltonian. The figure coming up the driveway was not Milton's Lucifer. It was the Devil.

My heart began to pound in my chest, to pound so hard that it hurt. I hoped it could not see me, that, in a dark house, behind window glass, I was hidden.

The figure flickered and changed as it walked up the drive. One moment it was dark, bull-like, Minotaurish, the next it was slim and female, and the next it was a cat itself, a scarred, huge gray-green wildcat, its face contorted with hate.

There are steps that lead up to my porch, four white wooden steps in need of a coat of paint (I knew they were white, although they were, like everything else, green through my binoculars). At the bottom of the steps, the Devil stopped and called out something that I could not understand, three, perhaps four words in a whining, howling language that must have been old and forgotten when Babylon was young; and, although I did not understand the words, I felt the hairs rise on the back of my head as it called.

And then I heard, muffled through the glass, but still audible, a low growl, a challenge, and—slowly, unsteadily—a black figure walked down the steps of the house, away from me, toward the Devil. These days the Black Cat no longer moved like a panther, instead he stumbled and rocked, like a sailor only recently returned to land.

The Devil was a woman now. She said something soothing and gentle to the cat, in a tongue that sounded like French, and reached out a hand to him. He sank his teeth into her arm, and her lip curled, and she spat at him.

The woman glanced up at me then, and if I had doubted that she was the Devil before, I was certain of it now: the woman's eyes flashed red fire at me, but you can see no red through the night-vision binoculars, only shades of a green. And the Devil saw me, through the window. It saw me. I am in no doubt about that at all.

The Devil twisted and writhed, and now it was some kind of jackal, a flat-faced, huge-headed, bull-necked creature, halfway between a hyena and a dingo. There were maggots squirming in its mangy fur, and it began to walk up the steps.

The Black Cat leapt upon it, and in seconds they became a rolling, writhing thing, moving faster than my eyes could follow.

All this in silence.

And then a low roar—down the country road at the bottom of our drive, in the distance, lumbered a late-night truck, its blazing headlights burning bright as green suns through the binoculars. I lowered them from my eyes and saw only darkness, and the gentle yellow of headlights, and then the red of rear lights as it vanished off again into the nowhere at all.

When I raised the binoculars once more, there was nothing to be seen. Only the Black Cat on the steps, staring up into the air. I trained the binoculars up and saw something flying away—a vulture, perhaps, or an eagle—and then it flew beyond the trees and was gone.

I went out onto the porch, and picked up the Black Cat, and stroked him, and said kind, soothing things to him. He mewled piteously when I first approached him, but, after a while, he went to sleep on my lap, and I put him into his basket, and went upstairs to my bed, to sleep myself. There was dried blood on my T-shirt and jeans, the following morning.

That was a week ago.

The thing that comes to my house does not come every night. But it comes most nights: we know it by the wounds on the cat, and the pain I can see in those leonine eyes. He has lost the use of his front left paw, and his right eye has closed for good.

I wonder what we did to deserve the Black Cat. I wonder who sent him. And, selfish and scared, I wonder how much more he has to give.

How to Talk to Girls at Parties

"COME ON," SAID VIC. "It'll be great."

"No, it won't," I said, although I'd lost this fight hours ago, and I knew it.

"It'll be brilliant," said Vic, for the hundredth time. "Girls! Girls! Girls!" He grinned with white teeth.

We both attended an all-boys' school in south London. While it would be a lie to say that we had no experience with girls—Vic seemed to have had many girlfriends, while I had kissed three of my sister's friends—it would, I think, be perfectly true to say that we both chiefly spoke to, interacted with, and only truly understood, other boys. Well, I did, anyway. It's hard to speak for someone else, and I've not seen Vic for thirty years. I'm not sure that I would know what to say to him now if I did.

We were walking the backstreets that used to twine in a grimy maze behind East Croydon station—a friend had told Vic about a party, and Vic was determined to go whether I liked it or not, and I didn't. But my parents were away that week at a conference, and I was Vic's guest at his house, so I was trailing along beside him.

"It'll be the same as it always is," I said. "After an hour you'll be off somewhere snogging the prettiest girl at the party, and I'll be in the kitchen listening to somebody's mum going on about politics or poetry or something."

"You just have to *talk* to them," he said. "I think it's probably that road at the end here." He gestured cheerfully, swinging the bag with the bottle in it.

"Don't you know?"

"Alison gave me directions and I wrote them on a bit of paper, but I left it on the hall table. S'okay. I can find it."

"How?" Hope welled slowly up inside me.

"We walk down the road," he said, as if speaking to an idiot child. "And we look for the party. Easy."

I looked, but saw no party: just narrow houses with rusting cars or bikes in their concreted front gardens; and the dusty glass fronts of newsagents, which smelled of alien spices and sold everything from birthday cards and secondhand comics to the kind of magazines that were so pornographic that they were sold already sealed in plastic bags. I had been there when Vic had slipped one of those magazines beneath his sweater, but the owner caught him on the pavement outside and made him give it back.

We reached the end of the road and turned into a narrow street of terraced houses. Everything looked very still and empty in the summer's evening. "It's all right for you," I said. "They fancy you. You don't actually *have* to talk to them." It was true: one urchin grin from Vic and he could have his pick of the room.

"Nah. S'not like that. You've just got to talk."

The times I had kissed my sister's friends I had not spoken to them. They had been around while my sister was off doing something elsewhere, and they had drifted into my orbit, and so I had kissed them. I do not remember any talking. I did not know what to say to girls, and I told him so.

"They're just girls," said Vic. "They don't come from another planet."

As we followed the curve of the road around, my

hopes that the party would prove unfindable began to fade: a low pulsing noise, music muffled by walls and doors, could be heard from a house up ahead. It was eight in the evening, not that early if you aren't yet sixteen, and we weren't. Not quite.

I had parents who liked to know where I was, but I don't think Vic's parents cared that much. He was the youngest of five boys. That in itself seemed magical to me: I merely had two sisters, both younger than I was, and I felt both unique and lonely. I had wanted a brother as far back as I could remember. When I turned thirteen, I stopped wishing on falling stars or first stars, but back when I did, a brother was what I had wished for.

We went up the garden path, crazy paving leading us past a hedge and a solitary rosebush to a pebble-dashed facade. We rang the doorbell, and the door was opened by a girl. I could not have told you how old she was, which was one of the things about girls I had begun to hate: when you start out as kids you're just boys and girls, going through time at the same speed, and you're all five, or seven, or eleven, together. And then one day there's a lurch and the girls just sort of sprint off into the future ahead of you, and they know all about everything, and they have periods and breasts and makeup and God only knew what else—for I certainly didn't. The diagrams in biology textbooks were no substitute for being, in a very real sense, young adults. And the girls of our age were.

Vic and I weren't young adults, and I was beginning to suspect that even when I started needing to shave every day, instead of once every couple of weeks, I would still be way behind.

The girl said, "Hello?"

Vic said, "We're friends of Alison's." We had met Alison, all freckles and orange hair and a wicked smile, in Hamburg, on a German exchange. The exchange organizers had sent some girls with us, from a local girls' school, to balance the sexes. The girls, our age, more or less, were raucous and funny, and had more or less adult boyfriends with cars and jobs and motorbikes and—in the case of one girl with crooked teeth and a raccoon coat, who spoke to me about it sadly at the end of a party in Hamburg, in, of course, the kitchen—a wife and kids.

"She isn't here," said the girl at the door. "No Alison."

"Not to worry," said Vic, with an easy grin. "I'm Vic. This is Enn." A beat, and then the girl smiled back at him. Vic had a bottle of white wine in a plastic bag, removed from his parents' kitchen cabinet. "Where should I put this, then?"

She stood out of the way, letting us enter. "There's a kitchen in the back," she said. "Put it on the table there, with the other bottles." She had golden, wavy hair, and she was very beautiful. The hall was dim in the twilight, but I could see that she was beautiful.

"What's your name, then?" said Vic.

She told him it was Stella, and he grinned his crooked white grin and told her that that had to be the prettiest name he had ever heard. Smooth bastard. And what was worse was that he said it like he meant it.

Vic headed back to drop off the wine in the kitchen, and I looked into the front room, where the music was coming from. There were people dancing in there. Stella walked in, and she started to dance, swaying to the music all alone, and I watched her.

This was during the early days of punk. On our own record players we would play the Adverts and the Jam, the Stranglers and the Clash and the Sex

Pistols. At other people's parties you'd hear ELO or 10cc or even Roxy Music. Maybe some Bowie, if you were lucky. During the German exchange, the only LP that we had all been able to agree on was Neil Young's *Harvest*, and his song "Heart of Gold" had threaded through the trip like a refrain: *I crossed the ocean for a heart of gold. . . .*

The music playing in that front room wasn't anything I recognized. It sounded a bit like a German electronic pop group called Kraftwerk, and a bit like an LP I'd been given for my last birthday, of strange sounds made by the BBC Radiophonic Workshop. The music had a beat, though, and the half-dozen girls in that room were moving gently to it, although I only looked at Stella. She shone.

Vic pushed past me, into the room. He was holding a can of lager. "There's booze back in the kitchen," he told me. He wandered over to Stella and he began to talk to her. I couldn't hear what they were saying over the music, but I knew that there was no room for me in that conversation.

I didn't like beer, not back then. I went off to see if there was something I wanted to drink. On the kitchen table stood a large bottle of Coca-Cola, and

I poured myself a plastic tumblerful, and I didn't dare say anything to the pair of girls who were talking in the underlit kitchen. They were animated and utterly lovely. Each of them had very black skin and glossy hair and movie star clothes, and their accents were foreign, and each of them was out of my league.

I wandered, Coke in hand.

The house was deeper than it looked, larger and more complex than the two-up two-down model I had imagined. The rooms were underlit—I doubt there was a bulb of more than 40 watts in the building—and each room I went into was inhabited: in my memory, inhabited only by girls. I did not go upstairs.

A girl was the only occupant of the conservatory. Her hair was so fair it was white, and long, and straight, and she sat at the glass-topped table, her hands clasped together, staring at the garden outside, and the gathering dusk. She seemed wistful.

"Do you mind if I sit here?" I asked, gesturing with my cup. She shook her head, and then followed it up with a shrug, to indicate that it was all the same to her. I sat down.

Vic walked past the conservatory door. He was talking to Stella, but he looked in at me, sitting at the table, wrapped in shyness and awkwardness, and he opened and closed his hand in a parody of a speaking mouth. *Talk*. Right.

"Are you from around here?" I asked the girl.

She shook her head. She wore a low-cut silvery top, and I tried not to stare at the swell of her breasts.

I said, "What's your name? I'm Enn."

"Wain's Wain," she said, or something that sounded like it. "I'm a second."

"That's, uh. That's a different name."

She fixed me with huge, liquid eyes. "It indicates that my progenitor was also Wain, and that I am obliged to report back to her. I may not breed."

"Ah. Well. Bit early for that anyway, isn't it?"

She unclasped her hands, raised them above the table, spread her fingers. "You see?" The little finger on her left hand was crooked, and it bifurcated at the top, splitting into two smaller fingertips. A minor deformity. "When I was finished a decision was needed. Would I be retained, or eliminated? I was fortunate that the decision was with me. Now, I travel, while my more perfect sisters remain at home in stasis. They were firsts. I am a second.

"Soon I must return to Wain, and tell her all I have seen. All my impressions of this place of yours."

"I don't actually live in Croydon," I said. "I don't come from here." I wondered if she was American. I had no idea what she was talking about.

"As you say," she agreed, "neither of us comes from here." She folded her six-fingered left hand beneath her right, as if tucking it out of sight. "I had expected it to be bigger, and cleaner, and more colorful. But still, it is a jewel."

She yawned, covered her mouth with her right hand, only for a moment, before putting it back on the table again. "I grow weary of the journeying, and I wish sometimes that it would end. On a street in Río, at Carnival, I saw them on a bridge, golden and tall and insect-eyed and winged, and elated I almost ran to greet them, before I saw that they were only people in costumes. I said to Hola Colt, 'Why do they try so hard to look like us?' and Hola Colt replied, 'Because they hate themselves, all shades of pink and brown, and so small.' It is what I experience, even me, and I am not grown. It is like a world of children, or of elves." Then she smiled, and said, "It was a good thing they could not any of them see Hola Colt."

"Um," I said, "do you want to dance?"

She shook her head immediately. "It is not permitted," she said. "I can do nothing that might cause damage to property. I am Wain's."

"Would you like something to drink, then?"

"Water," she said.

I went back to the kitchen and poured myself another Coke, and filled a cup with water from the tap. From the kitchen back to the hall, and from there into the conservatory, but now it was quite empty.

I wondered if the girl had gone to the toilet, and if she might change her mind about dancing later. I walked back to the front room and stared in. The place was filling up. There were more girls dancing, and several lads I didn't know, who looked a few years older than me and Vic. The lads and the girls all kept their distance, but Vic was holding Stella's hand as they danced, and when the song ended he put an arm around her, casually, almost proprietorially, to make sure that nobody else cut in.

I wondered if the girl I had been talking to in the conservatory was now upstairs, as she did not appear to be on the ground floor.

I walked into the living room, which was across the hall from the room where the people were dancing, and I sat down on the sofa. There was a girl sitting there already. She had dark hair, cut short and spiky, and a nervous manner.

Talk, I thought. "Um, this mug of water's going spare," I told her, "if you want it?"

She nodded, and reached out her hand and took the mug extremely carefully, as if she were unused to taking things, as if she could trust neither her vision nor her hands.

"I love being a tourist," she said, and smiled hesitantly. She had a gap between her two front teeth, and she sipped the tap water as if she were an adult sipping a fine wine. "The last tour, we went to sun, and we swam in sunfire pools with the whales. We heard their histories and we shivered in the chill of the outer places, then we swam deepward where the heat churned and comforted us.

"I wanted to go back. This time, I wanted it. There

was so much I had not seen. Instead we came to world. Do you like it?"

"Like what?"

She gestured vaguely to the room—the sofa, the armchairs, the curtains, the unused gas fire.

"It's all right, I suppose."

"I told them I did not wish to visit world," she said. "My parent-teacher was unimpressed. 'You will have much to learn,' it told me. I said, 'I could learn more in sun, again. Or in the deeps. Jessa spun webs between galaxies. I want to do that.'

"But there was no reasoning with it, and I came to world. Parent-teacher engulfed me, and I was here, embodied in a decaying lump of meat hanging on a frame of calcium. As I incarnated I felt things deep inside me, fluttering and pumping and squishing. It was my first experience with pushing air through the mouth, vibrating the vocal cords on the way, and I used it to tell parent-teacher that I wished that I would die, which it acknowledged was the inevitable exit strategy from world."

There were black worry beads wrapped around her wrist, and she fiddled with them as she spoke. "But knowledge is there, in the meat," she said, "and

I am resolved to learn from it."

We were sitting close at the center of the sofa now. I decided I should put an arm around her, but casually. I would extend my arm along the back of the sofa and eventually sort of creep it down, almost imperceptibly, until it was touching her. She said, "The thing with the liquid in the eyes, when the world blurs. Nobody told me, and I still do not understand. I have touched the folds of the Whisper and pulsed and flown with the tachyon swans, and I still do not understand."

She wasn't the prettiest girl there, but she seemed nice enough, and she was a girl, anyway. I let my arm slide down a little, tentatively, so that it made contact with her back, and she did not tell me to take it away.

Vic called to me then, from the doorway. He was standing with his arm around Stella, protectively, waving at me. I tried to let him know, by shaking my head, that I was onto something, but he called my name and, reluctantly, I got up from the sofa and walked over to the door. "What?"

"Er. Look. The party," said Vic apologetically. "It's not the one I thought it was. I've been talking to

Stella and I figured it out. Well, she sort of explained it to me. We're at a different party."

"Christ. Are we in trouble? Do we have to go?"

Stella shook her head. He leaned down and kissed her, gently, on the lips. "You're just happy to have me here, aren't you darlin'?"

"You know I am," she told him.

He looked from her back to me, and he smiled his white smile: roguish, lovable, a little bit Artful Dodger, a little bit wide-boy Prince Charming. "Don't worry. They're all tourists here anyway. It's a foreign exchange thing, innit? Like when we all went to Germany."

"It is?"

"Enn. You got to *talk* to them. And that means you got to listen to them, too. You understand?"

"I *did*. I already talked to a couple of them."

"You getting anywhere?"

"I was till you called me over."

"Sorry about that. Look, I just wanted to fill you in. Right?"

And he patted my arm and he walked away with Stella. Then, together, the two of them went up the stairs.

Understand me, all the girls at that party, in the twilight, were lovely; they all had perfect faces but, more important than that, they had whatever strangeness of proportion, of oddness or humanity it is that makes a beauty something more than a shop window dummy. Stella was the most lovely of any of them, but she, of course, was Vic's, and they were going upstairs together, and that was just how things would always be.

There were several people now sitting on the sofa, talking to the gap-toothed girl. Someone told a joke, and they all laughed. I would have had to push my way in there to sit next to her again, and it didn't look like she was expecting me back or cared that I had gone, so I wandered out into the hall. I glanced in at the dancers, and found myself wondering where the music was coming from. I couldn't see a record player or speakers.

From the hall I walked back to the kitchen.

Kitchens are good at parties. You never need an excuse to be there, and, on the good side, at this party I couldn't see any signs of someone's mum. I inspected the various bottles and cans on the kitchen table, then I poured a half an inch of Pernod into the bottom of my plastic cup, which I filled to the top with Coke. I dropped in a couple of ice cubes and took a sip, relishing the sweet-shop tang of the drink.

"What's that you're drinking?" A girl's voice.

"It's Pernod," I told her. "It tastes like aniseed balls, only it's alcoholic." I didn't say that I only tried it because I'd heard someone in the crowd ask for a Pernod on a live Velvet Underground LP.

"Can I have one?" I poured another Pernod, topped it off with Coke, passed it to her. Her hair was a coppery auburn, and it tumbled around her head in ringlets. It's not a hairstyle you see much now, but you saw it a lot back then.

"What's your name?" I asked.

"Triolet," she said.

"Pretty name," I told her, although I wasn't sure that it was. She was pretty, though.

"It's a verse form," she said proudly. "Like me."

"You're a poem?"

She smiled, and looked down and away, perhaps bashfully. Her profile was almost flat—a perfect Grecian nose that came down from her forehead in a straight line. We did *Antigone* in the school theater the previous year. I was the messenger who brings Creon the news of Antigone's death. We wore half-masks that made us look like that. I thought of that play, looking at her face, in the kitchen, and I thought of Barry Smith's drawings of women in the *Conan* comics: five years later I would have thought of the Pre-Raphaelites, of Jane Morris and Lizzie Siddall. But I was only fifteen then.

"You're a poem?" I repeated.

She chewed her lower lip. "If you want. I am a poem, or I am a pattern, or a race of people whose world was swallowed by the sea."

"Isn't it hard to be three things at the same time?"

"What's your name?"

"Enn."

"So you are Enn," she said. "And you are a male. And you are a biped. Is it hard to be three things at the same time?"

"But they aren't different things. I mean, they aren't contradictory." It was a word I had read many times but never said aloud before that night, and I put the stresses in the wrong places. *Contradictory.*

She wore a thin dress made of a white, silky fabric. Her eyes were a pale green, a color that would now make me think of tinted contact lenses; but this was thirty years ago; things were different then. I remember wondering about Vic and Stella, upstairs. By now, I was sure that they were in one of the bedrooms, and I envied Vic so much it almost hurt.

Still, I was talking to this girl, even if we were talking nonsense, even if her name wasn't really Triolet (my generation had not been given hippie names: all the Rainbows and the Sunshines and the Moons, they were only six, seven, eight years old back then). She said, "We knew that it would soon be over, and so we put it all into a poem, to tell the universe who we were, and why we were here, and what we said and did and thought and dreamed and yearned for. We wrapped our dreams in words and patterned the words so that they would live forever, unforgettable. Then we sent the poem as a pattern of flux, to wait in the heart of a star, beaming out its message in pulses and bursts and fuzzes across the electromagnetic spectrum, until the time when, on worlds a thousand sun systems distant, the pattern would be decoded and read, and it would become a poem once again."

"And then what happened?"

She looked at me with her green eyes, and it was as if she stared out at me from her own Antigone half-mask; but as if her pale green eyes were just a different, deeper, part of the mask. "You cannot hear a poem without it changing you," she told me. "They heard it, and it colonized them. It inherited them and it inhabited them, its rhythms becoming part of the way that they thought; its images permanently transmuting their metaphors; its verses, its outlook, its aspirations becoming their lives. Within a generation their children would be born already knowing the poem, and, sooner rather than later, as these things go, there were no more children born. There was no need for them, not any longer. There was only a poem, which took flesh and walked and spread itself across the vastness of the known."

I edged closer to her, so I could feel my leg pressing against hers. She seemed to welcome it: she put her hand on my arm, affectionately, and I felt a smile spreading across my face.

"There are places that we are welcomed," said Triolet, "and places where we are regarded as a noxious weed, or as a disease, something immediately to be quarantined and eliminated. But where

158

does contagion end and art begin?"

"I don't know," I said, still smiling. I could hear the unfamiliar music as it pulsed and scattered and boomed in the front room.

She leaned into me then and—I suppose it was a kiss. . . . I suppose. She pressed her lips to my lips, anyway, and then, satisfied, she pulled back, as if she had now marked me as her own.

"Would you like to hear it?" she asked, and I nodded, unsure what she was offering me, but certain that I needed anything she was willing to give.

She began to whisper something in my ear. It's the strangest thing about poetry—you can tell it's poetry, even if you don't speak the language. You can hear Homer's Greek without understanding a word, and you still know it's poetry. I've heard Polish poetry, and Inuit poetry, and I knew what it was without knowing. Her whisper was like that. I didn't know the language, but her words washed through me, perfect, and in my mind's eye I saw towers of glass and diamond; and people with eyes of the palest green; and, unstoppable, beneath every syllable, I could feel the relentless advance of the ocean.

Perhaps I kissed her properly. I don't remember. I know I wanted to.

And then Vic was shaking me violently. "Come on!" he was shouting. "Quickly. Come on!"

In my head I began to come back from a thousand miles away.

"Idiot. Come on. Just get a move on," he said, and he swore at me. There was fury in his voice.

For the first time that evening I recognized one of the songs being played in the front room. A sad saxophone wail followed by a cascade of liquid chords, a man's voice singing cut-up lyrics about the sons of the silent age. I wanted to stay and hear the song.

She said, "I am not finished. There is yet more of me."

"Sorry, love," said Vic, but he wasn't smiling any longer. "There'll be another time," and he grabbed me by the elbow and he twisted and pulled, forcing me from the room. I did not resist. I knew from experience that Vic could beat the stuffing out of me if he got it into his head to do so. He wouldn't do it unless he was upset or angry, but he was angry now.

Out into the front hall. As Vic pulled open the door, I looked back one last time, over my shoulder, hoping to see Triolet in the doorway to the kitchen, but she was not there. I saw Stella, though, at the top of the stairs. She was staring down at Vic, and I saw her face.

This all happened thirty years ago. I have forgotten much, and I will forget more, and in the end I will forget everything; yet, if I have any certainty of life beyond death, it is all wrapped up not in psalms or hymns, but in this one thing alone: I cannot believe that I will ever forget that moment, or forget the expression on Stella's face as she watched Vic hurrying away from her. Even in death I shall remember that.

Her clothes were in disarray, and there was make-up smudged across her face, and her eyes—

You wouldn't want to make a universe angry. I bet an angry universe would look at you with eyes like that.

We ran then, me and Vic, away from the party and the tourists and the twilight, ran as if a lightning storm was on our heels, a mad helter-skelter dash down the confusion of streets, threading through the maze, and we did not look back, and we did not stop until we could not breathe; and then we stopped and panted, unable to run any longer. We were in pain. I held on to a wall, and Vic threw up, hard and long, into the gutter.

He wiped his mouth.

"She wasn't a—" He stopped.

He shook his head.

Then he said, "You know . . . I think there's a thing. When you've gone as far as you dare. And if you go any further, you wouldn't be *you* anymore? You'd be the person who'd done *that*? The places you just can't go. . . . I think that happened to me tonight."

I thought I knew what he was saying. "Screw her, you mean?" I said.

He rammed a knuckle hard against my temple, and twisted it violently. I wondered if I was going to have to fight him—and lose—but after a moment he lowered his hand and moved away from me, making a low, gulping noise.

I looked at him curiously, and I realized that he was crying: his face was scarlet; snot and tears ran down his cheeks. Vic was sobbing in the street, as unself-consciously and heartbreakingly as a little boy. He walked away from me then, shoulders heaving, and he hurried down the road so he was in front of me and I could no longer see his face. I wondered what had occurred in that upstairs room to make him behave like that, to scare him so, and I could not even begin to guess.

The streetlights came on, one by one; Vic stumbled on ahead, while I trudged down the street behind him in the dusk, my feet treading out the measure of a poem that, try as I might, I could not properly remember and would never be able to repeat.

Sunbird

THEY WERE A RICH and a rowdy bunch at the
Epicurean Club in those days. They certainly
knew how to party. There were five of them:
There was Augustus TwoFeathers McCoy, big
enough for three men, who ate enough for four
men and who drank enough for five. His great-
grandfather had founded the Epicurean Club with
the proceeds of a tontine, which he had taken great
pains, in the traditional manner, to ensure that he
had collected in full.

There was Professor Mandalay, small and twitchy
and gray as a ghost (and perhaps he was a ghost;
stranger things have happened), who drank nothing
but water and who ate doll portions from plates the
size of saucers. Still, you do not need the gusto for
the gastronomy, and Mandalay always got to the
heart of every dish placed in front of him.

There was Virginia Boote, the food and restaurant

critic, who had once been a great beauty but was now a grand and magnificent ruin, and who delighted in her ruination.

There was Jackie Newhouse, the descendant (on the left-handed route) of the great lover, gourmand, violinist, and duelist Giacomo Casanova. Jackie Newhouse had, like his notorious ancestor, both broken his share of hearts and eaten his share of great dishes.

And there was Zebediah T. Crawcrustle, who was the only one of the Epicureans who was flat-out broke: he shambled in unshaven from the street when they had their meetings, with half a bottle of rotgut in a brown paper bag, hatless and coatless and, too often, partly shirtless, but he ate with more of an appetite than any of them.

Augustus TwoFeathers McCoy was talking—

"We have eaten everything that can be eaten," said Augustus TwoFeathers McCoy, and there was regret and glancing sorrow in his voice. "We have eaten vulture, mole, and fruit bat."

Mandalay consulted his notebook. "Vulture tasted like rotten pheasant. Mole tasted like carrion slug. Fruit bat tasted remarkably like sweet guinea pig."

"We have eaten kakapo, aye-aye, and giant panda—"

"Oh, that broiled panda steak," sighed Virginia Boote, her mouth watering at the memory.

"We have eaten several long-extinct species," said Augustus TwoFeathers McCoy. "We have eaten flash-frozen mammoth and Patagonian giant sloth."

"If we had but gotten to the mammoth a little faster," sighed Jackie Newhouse. "I could tell why the hairy elephants went so fast, though, once people got a taste of them. I am a man of elegant pleasures, but after only one bite, I found myself thinking only of Kansas City barbecue sauce and what the ribs on those things would be like, if they were fresh."

"Nothing wrong with being on ice for a millennium or two," said Zebediah T. Crawcrustle. He grinned. His teeth may have been crooked, but they were sharp and strong. "Even so, for real taste you had to go for honest-to-goodness mastodon every time. Mammoth was always what people settled for, when they couldn't get mastodon."

"We've eaten squid, and giant squid, and humongous squid," said Augustus TwoFeathers McCoy.

"We've eaten lemmings and Tasmanian tigers. We've eaten bowerbird and ortolan and peacock. We've eaten the dolphin fish (which is not the mammal dolphin) and the giant sea turtle and the Sumatran rhino. We've eaten everything there is to eat."

"Nonsense. There are many hundreds of things we have not yet tasted," said Professor Mandalay. "Thousands, perhaps. Think of all the species of beetle there are, still untasted."

"Oh Mandy," sighed Virginia Boote. "When you've tasted one beetle, you've tasted them all. And we all tasted several hundred species. At least the dung beetles had a real kick to them."

"No," said Jackie Newhouse, "that was the dung-beetle balls. The beetles themselves were singularly unexceptional. Still, I take your point. We have scaled the heights of gastronomy, we have plunged down into the depths of gustation. We have become cosmonauts exploring undreamed of worlds of delectation and gourmanderie."

"True, true, true," said Augustus TwoFeathers McCoy. "There has been a meeting of the Epicureans every month for over a hundred and fifty years, in my father's time, and my grandfather's time, and my great-grandfather's time, and now I fear that I must hang it up for there is nothing left that we, or our predecessors in the club, have not eaten."

"I wish I had been here in the twenties," said Virginia Boote, "when they legally had Man on the menu."

"Only after it had been electrocuted," said Zebediah T. Crawcrustle. "Half-fried already it was, all char and crackling. It left none of us with a taste for long pig, save one who was already that way inclined, and he went out pretty soon after that anyway."

"Oh, Crusty, *why* must you pretend that you were there?" asked Virginia Boote, with a yawn. "Anyone can see you aren't that old. You can't be more than sixty, even allowing for the ravages of time and the gutter."

"Oh, they ravage pretty good," said Zebediah T. Crawcrustle. "But not as good as you'd imagine. Anyway there's a host of things we've not eaten yet."

"Name one," said Mandalay, his pencil poised precisely above his notebook.

EPICUREAN CLUB.

"Well, there's Suntown Sunbird," said Zebediah T. Crawcrustle. And he grinned his crookedy grin at them, with his teeth ragged but sharp.

"I've never heard of it," said Jackie Newhouse. "You're making it up."

"I've heard of it," said Professor Mandalay, "but in another context. And besides, it is imaginary."

"Unicorns are imaginary," said Virginia Boote, "but, gosh, that unicorn flank tartare was tasty. A little bit horsey, a little bit goatish, and all the better for the capers and raw quail eggs."

"There's something about the Sunbird in one of the minutes of the Epicurean Club from bygone years," said Augustus TwoFeathers McCoy. "But what it was, I can no longer remember."

"Did they say how it tasted?" asked Virginia.

"I do not believe that they did," said Augustus, with a frown. "I would need to inspect the bound proceedings, of course."

"Nah," said Zebediah T. Crawcrustle. "That's only in the charred volumes. You'll never find out about it from there."

Augustus TwoFeathers McCoy scratched his head. He really did have two feathers, which went through the knot of black hair shot with silver at the back of his head, and the feathers had once been golden although by now they were looking kind of ordinary and yellow and ragged. He had been given them when he was a boy.

"Beetles," said Professor Mandalay. "I once calculated that, if a man such as myself were to eat six different species of beetle each day, it would take him more than twenty years to eat every beetle that has been identified. And over that twenty years enough new species of beetle might have been discovered to keep him eating for another five years. And in those five years enough beetles might have been discovered to keep him eating for another two and a half years, and so on, and so on. It is a paradox of inexhaustibility. I call it Mandalay's Beetle. You would have to enjoy eating beetles, though," he added, "or it would be a very bad thing indeed."

"Nothing wrong with eating beetles if they're the right kind of beetle," said Zebediah T. Crawcrustle. "Right now, I've got a hankering on me for lightning bugs. There's a kick from the glow of a lightning bug that might be just what I need."

"While the lightning bug or firefly (*Photinus*

pyralis) is more of a beetle than it is a glowworm," said Mandalay, "it is by no stretch of the imagination edible."

"They may not be edible," said Crawcrustle, "but they'll get you into shape for the stuff that is. I think I'll roast me some. Fireflies and habañero peppers. Yum."

Virginia Boote was an eminently practical woman. She said, "Suppose we did want to eat Suntown Sunbird. Where should we start looking for it?"

Zebediah T. Crawcrustle scratched the bristling seventh-day beard that was sprouting on his chin (it never grew any longer than that; seventh-day beards never do). "If it was me," he told them, "I'd head down to Suntown of a noon in midsummer, and I'd find somewhere comfortable to sit—Mustapha Stroheim's coffeehouse, for example—and I'd wait for the Sunbird to come by. Then I'd catch him in the traditional manner, and cook him in the traditional manner as well."

"And what would the traditional manner of catching him be?" asked Jackie Newhouse.

"Why, the same way your famous ancestor

poached quails and wood grouse," said Crawcrustle.

"There's nothing in Casanova's memoirs about poaching quail," said Jackie Newhouse.

"Your ancestor was a busy man," said Crawcrustle. "He couldn't be expected to write everything down. But he poached a good quail nonetheless."

"Dried corn and dried blueberries, soaked in whiskey," said Augustus TwoFeathers McCoy. "That's how my folk always did it."

"And that was how Casanova did it," said Crawcrustle, "although he used barley grains mixed with raisins, and he soaked the raisins in brandy. He taught me himself."

Jackie Newhouse ignored this statement. It was easy to ignore much that Zebediah T. Crawcrustle said. Instead, Jackie Newhouse asked, "And where is Mustapha Stroheim's coffeehouse in Suntown?"

"Why, where it always is, third lane after the old market in the Suntown district, just before you reach the old drainage ditch that was once an irrigation canal, and if you find yourself outside One-eye Khayam's carpet shop you have gone too far," began Crawcrustle. "But I see by the expressions of irritation upon your faces that you were expecting a less succinct, less accurate description. Very well. It is in Suntown, and Suntown is in Cairo, in Egypt, where it always is, or almost always."

"And who will pay for an expedition to Suntown?" asked Augustus TwoFeathers McCoy. "And who will be on this expedition? I ask the question although I already know the answer, and I do not like it."

"Why, you will pay for it, Augustus, and we will all come," said Zebediah T. Crawcrustle. "You can deduct it from our Epicurean membership dues. And I shall bring my chef's apron and my cooking utensils."

Augustus knew that Crawcrustle had not paid his Epicurean Club membership in much too long a time, but the Epicurean Club would cover him; Crawcrustle had been a member of the Epicureans in Augustus's father's day. He simply said, "And when shall we leave?"

Crawcrustle fixed him with a mad old eye and shook his head in disappointment. "Why, Augustus," he said. "We're going to Suntown, to catch the Sunbird. When else should we leave?"

"Sunday!" sang Virginia Boote. "Darlings, we'll

leave on a Sunday!"

"There's hope for you yet, young lady," said Zebediah T. Crawcrustle. "We shall leave Sunday indeed. Three Sundays from now. And we shall travel to Egypt. We shall spend several days hunting and trapping the elusive Sunbird of Suntown, and, finally, we shall deal with it in the traditional way."

Professor Mandalay blinked a small gray blink. "But," he said, "I am teaching a class on Monday. On Mondays I teach mythology, on Tuesdays I teach tap dancing, and on Wednesdays, woodwork."

"Get a teaching assistant to take your course, Mandalay, O Mandalay. On Monday you'll be hunting the Sunbird," said Zebediah T. Crawcrustle. "And how many other professors can say that?"

They went, one by one, to see Crawcrustle, in order to discuss the journey ahead of them, and to announce their misgivings.

Zebediah T. Crawcrustle was a man of no fixed abode. Still, there were places he could be found, if you were of a mind to find him. In the early mornings he slept in the bus terminal, where the benches were comfortable and the transport police were inclined to let him lie; in the heat of the afternoons he hung in the park by the statues of long-forgotten generals, with the dipsos and the winos and the hop-heads, sharing their company and the contents of their bottles, and offering his opinion, which was, as that of an Epicurean, always considered and always respected, if not always welcomed.

Augustus TwoFeathers McCoy sought out Crawcrustle in the park; he had with him his daughter, Hollyberry NoFeathers McCoy. She was small, but she was sharp as a shark's tooth.

"You know," said Augustus, "there is something very familiar about this."

"About what?" asked Zebediah.

"All of this. The expedition to Egypt. The Sunbird. It seemed to me like I heard about it before."

Crawcrustle merely nodded. He was crunching something from a brown paper bag.

Augustus said, "I went to the bound annals of the Epicurean Club, and I looked it up. And there was what I took to be a reference to the Sunbird in the index for forty years ago, but I was unable to learn anything more."

"And why was that?" asked Zebediah T.

Crawcrustle, swallowing noisily.

Augustus TwoFeathers McCoy sighed. "I found the relevant page in the annals," he said, "but it was burned away, and afterward there was some great confusion in the administration of the Epicurean Club."

"You're eating lightning bugs from a paper bag," said Hollyberry NoFeathers McCoy. "I seen you doing it."

"I am indeed, little lady," said Zebediah T. Crawcrustle.

"Do you remember the days of great confusion, Crawcrustle?" asked Augustus.

"I do indeed," said Crawcrustle. "And I remember you. You were only the age that young Hollyberry is now. But there is always confusion, Augustus, and then there is no confusion. It is like the rising and the setting of the sun."

Jackie Newhouse and Professor Mandalay found Crawcrustle that evening, behind the railroad tracks. He was roasting something in a tin can over a small charcoal fire.

"What are you roasting, Crawcrustle?" asked Jackie Newhouse.

"More charcoal," said Crawcrustle. "Cleans the blood, purifies the spirit."

There was basswood and hickory, cut up into little chunks at the bottom of the can, all black and smoking.

"And will you actually eat this charcoal, Crawcrustle?" asked Professor Mandalay.

In response, Crawcrustle licked his fingers and picked out a lump of charcoal from the can. It hissed and fizzed in his grip.

"A fine trick," said Professor Mandalay. "That's how fire-eaters do it, I believe."

Crawcrustle popped the charcoal into his mouth and crunched it between his ragged old teeth. "It is indeed," he said. "It is indeed."

Jackie Newhouse cleared his throat. "The truth of the matter is," he said, "Professor Mandalay and I have deep misgivings about the journey that lies ahead."

Zebediah merely crunched his charcoal. "Not hot enough," he said. He took a stick from the fire and nibbled off the orange-hot tip of it. "That's good," he said.

"It's all an illusion," said Jackie Newhouse.

"Nothing of the sort," said Zebediah T. Crawcrustle primly. "It's prickly elm."

"I have extreme misgivings about all this," said Jackie Newhouse. "My ancestors and I have a finely tuned sense of personal preservation, one that has often left us shivering on roofs and hiding in rivers—one step away from the law, or from gentlemen with guns and legitimate grievances—and that sense of self-preservation is telling me not to go to Suntown with you."

"I am an academic," said Professor Mandalay, "and thus have no finely developed senses that would be comprehensible to anyone who has not ever needed to grade papers without actually reading the blessed things. Still, I find the whole thing remarkably suspicious. If this Sunbird is so tasty, why have I not heard of it?"

"You have, Mandy old fruit. You have," said Zebediah T. Crawcrustle.

"And I am, in addition, an expert on geographical features from Tulsa, Oklahoma, to Timbuktu," continued Professor Mandalay. "Yet I have never seen a mention in any book of a place called Suntown in Cairo."

"Seen it mentioned? Why, you've taught it," said Crawcrustle, and he doused a lump of smoking charcoal with hot pepper sauce before popping it in his mouth and chomping it down.

"I don't believe you're really eating that," said Jackie Newhouse. "But even being around the trick of it is making me uncomfortable. I think it is time that I was elsewhere."

And he left. Perhaps Professor Mandalay left with him: that man was so gray and so ghostie it was always a toss-up whether he was there or not.

Virginia Boote tripped over Zebediah T. Crawcrustle while he rested in her doorway, in the small hours of the morning. She was returning from a restaurant she had needed to review. She got out of a taxi, tripped over Crawcrustle, and went sprawling. She landed nearby. "Whee!" she said. "That was some trip, wasn't it?"

"Indeed it was, Virginia," said Zebediah T. Crawcrustle. "You would not happen to have such a thing as a box of matches on you, would you?"

"I have a book of matches on me somewhere," she said, and she began to rummage in her purse, which was very large and very brown. "Here you are."

Zebediah T. Crawcrustle was carrying a bottle of purple methylated spirits, which he proceeded to pour into a plastic cup.

"Meths?" said Virginia Boote. "Somehow you never struck me as a meths drinker, Zebby."

"Nor am I," said Crawcrustle. "Foul stuff. It rots the guts and spoils the taste buds. But I could not find any lighter fluid at this time of night."

He lit a match, then dipped it near the surface of the cup of spirits, which began to burn with a flickery light. He ate the match. Then he gargled with the flaming liquid, and blew a sheet of flame into the street, incinerating a sheet of newspaper as it blew by.

"Crusty," said Virginia Boote, "that's a good way to get yourself killed."

Zebediah T. Crawcrustle grinned through black teeth. "I don't actually drink it," he told her. "I just gargle and breathe it out."

"You're playing with fire," she warned him.

"That's how I know I'm alive," said Zebediah T. Crawcrustle.

Virginia said, "Oh, Zeb. I *am* excited. I am so excited. What do you think the Sunbird tastes like?"

"Richer than quail and moister than turkey, fatter than ostrich and lusher than duck," said Zebediah T. Crawcrustle. "Once eaten it's never forgotten."

"We're going to Egypt," she said. "I've never been to Egypt." Then she said, "Do you have anywhere to stay the night?"

He coughed, a small cough that rattled around in his old chest. "I'm getting too old to sleep in doorways and gutters," he said. "Still, I have my pride."

"Well," she said, looking at the man, "you could sleep on my sofa."

"It is not that I am not grateful for the offer," he said, "but there is a bench in the bus station that has my name on it."

And he pushed himself away from the wall and tottered majestically down the street.

There really *was* a bench in the bus station that had his name on it. He had donated the bench to the bus station back when he was flush, and his name was attached to the back of it, engraved upon a small brass plaque. Zebediah T. Crawcrustle was not always poor. Sometimes he was rich, but he had difficulty in holding on to his wealth, and whenever he had become wealthy he discovered that the world frowned on rich men eating in hobo jungles at the back of the railroad, or consorting with the winos in the park, so he would fritter his wealth away as best he could. There were always little bits of it here and there that he had forgotten about, and sometimes he would forget that he did not like being rich, and then he would set out again and seek his fortune, and find it.

He had needed a shave for a week, and the hairs of his seven-day beard were starting to come through snow white.

They left for Egypt on a Sunday, the Epicureans. There were five of them there, and Hollyberry NoFeathers McCoy waved good-bye to them at the airport. It was a very small airport, which still permitted waves good-bye.

"Good-bye, Father!" called Hollyberry NoFeathers McCoy.

Augustus TwoFeathers McCoy waved back at her as they walked along the asphalt to the little prop plane, which would begin the first leg of their journey.

"It seems to me," said Augustus TwoFeathers

McCoy, "that I remember, albeit dimly, a day like this long, long ago. I was a small boy, in that memory, waving good-bye. I believe it was the last time I saw my father, and I am struck once more with a sudden presentiment of doom." He waved one last time at the small child at the other end of the field, and she waved back at him.

"You waved just as enthusiastically back then," agreed Zebediah T. Crawcrustle, "but I think she waves with slightly more aplomb."

It was true. She did.

They took a small plane and then a larger plane, then a smaller plane, a blimp, a gondola, a train, a hot-air balloon, and a rented Jeep.

They rattled through Cairo in the Jeep. They passed the old market, and they turned off on the third lane they came to (if they had continued on they would have come to a drainage ditch that was once an irrigation canal). Mustapha Stroheim himself was sitting outside in the street, perched on an elderly wicker chair. All of the tables and chairs were on the side of the street, and it was not a particularly wide street.

"Welcome, my friends, to my *kahwa*," said

Mustapha Stroheim. "*Kahwa* is Egyptian for café or for coffeehouse. Would you like tea? Or a game of dominoes?"

"We would like to be shown to our rooms," said Jackie Newhouse.

"Not me," said Zebediah T. Crawcrustle. "I'll sleep in the street. It's warm enough, and that doorstep over there looks mighty comfortable."

"I'll have coffee, please," said Augustus TwoFeathers McCoy.

"Of course."

"Do you have water?" asked Professor Mandalay.

"Who said that?" said Mustapha Stroheim. "Oh, it was you, little gray man. My mistake. When I first saw you I thought you were someone's shadow."

"I will have *shay sokkar bosta*," said Virginia Boote, which is a glass of hot tea with the sugar on the side. "And I will play backgammon with anyone who wishes to take me on. There's not a soul in Cairo I cannot beat at backgammon, if I can remember the rules."

Augustus TwoFeathers McCoy was shown to his room. Professor Mandalay was shown to his room.

Jackie Newhouse was shown to his room. This was not a lengthy procedure; they were all in the same room, after all. There was another room in the back where Virginia would sleep, and a third room for Mustapha Stroheim and his family.

"What's that you're writing?" asked Jackie Newhouse.

"It's the procedures, annals, and minutes of the Epicurean Club," said Professor Mandalay. He was writing in a large leather-bound book with a small black pen. "I have chronicled our journey here, and all the things that we have eaten on the way. I shall keep writing as we eat the Sunbird, to record for posterity all the tastes and textures, all the smells and the juices."

"Did Crawcrustle say how he was going to cook the Sunbird?" asked Jackie Newhouse.

"He did," said Augustus TwoFeathers McCoy. "He says that he will drain a beer can, so it is only a third full. And then he will add herbs and spices to the beer can. He will stand the bird up on the can, with the can in its inner cavity, and place it up on the barbecue to roast. He says it is the traditional way."

Jackie Newhouse sniffed. "It sounds suspiciously modern to me."

"Crawcrustle says it is the traditional method of cooking the Sunbird," repeated Augustus.

"Indeed I did," said Crawcrustle, coming up the stairs. It was a small building. The stairs weren't that far away, and the walls were not thick ones. "The oldest beer in the world is Egyptian beer, and they've been cooking the Sunbird with it for over five thousand years now."

"But the beer can is a relatively modern invention," said Professor Mandalay, as Zebediah T. Crawcrustle came through the door. Crawcrustle was holding a cup of Turkish coffee, black as tar, which steamed like a kettle and bubbled like a tar pit.

"That coffee looks pretty hot," said Augustus TwoFeathers McCoy.

Crawcrustle knocked back the cup, draining half the contents. "Nah," he said. "Not really. And the beer can isn't really that new an invention. We used to make them out of an amalgam of copper and tin in the old days, sometimes with a little silver in there, sometimes not. It depended on the smith, and what he had to hand. You needed something that would stand up to the heat. I see that you are all looking at me doubtfully. Gentlemen, consider: of course the ancient Egyptians made beer cans; where else would they have kept their beer?"

From outside the window, at the tables in the street, came a wailing, in many voices. Virginia Boote had persuaded the locals to start playing backgammon for money, and she was cleaning them out. That woman was a backgammon shark.

Out back of Mustapha Stroheim's coffeehouse there was a courtyard containing a broken-down old barbecue, made of clay bricks and a half-melted metal grating, and an old wooden table. Crawcrustle spent the next day rebuilding the barbecue and cleaning it, oiling down the metal grille.

"That doesn't look like it's been used in forty years," said Virginia Boote. Nobody would play backgammon with her any longer, and her purse bulged with grubby piasters.

"Something like that," said Crawcrustle. "Maybe a little more. Here, Ginnie, make yourself useful. I've written a list of things I need from the market. It's mostly herbs and spices and wood chips. You can take one of the children of Mustapha Stroheim to translate for you."

"My pleasure, Crusty."

The other three members of the Epicurean Club were occupying themselves in their own way. Jackie Newhouse was making friends with many of the people of the area, who were attracted by his elegant suits and his skill at playing the violin. Augustus TwoFeathers McCoy went for long walks. Professor Mandalay spent time translating the hieroglyphics he had noticed were incised upon the clay bricks in the barbecue. He said that a foolish man might believe that they proved the barbecue in Mustapha Stroheim's backyard was once sacred to the Sun. "But I, who am an intelligent man," he said, "I see immediately that what has happened is that bricks that were once, long ago, part of a temple, have, over the millennia, been reused. I doubt that these people know the value of what they have here."

"Oh, they know all right," said Zebediah T. Crawcrustle. "And these bricks weren't part of any temple. They've been right here for five thousand years, since we built the barbecue. Before that we made do with stones."

Virginia Boote returned with a filled shopping basket. "Here," she said. "Red sandalwood and patchouli, vanilla beans, lavender twigs and sage and cinnamon leaves, whole nutmegs, garlic bulbs, cloves, and rosemary: everything you wanted and more."

Zebediah T. Crawcrustle grinned with delight. "The Sunbird will be so happy," he told her.

He spent the afternoon preparing a barbecue sauce. He said it was only respectful, and besides, the Sunbird's flesh was often slightly on the dry side.

The Epicureans spent that evening sitting at the wicker tables in the street out front, while Mustapha Stroheim and his family brought them tea and coffee and hot mint drinks. Zebediah T. Crawcrustle had told the Epicureans that they would be having the Sunbird of Suntown for Sunday lunch, and that they might wish to avoid food the night before, to ensure that they had an appetite.

"I have a presentiment of doom upon me," said Augustus Two-Feathers McCoy that night, in a bed that was far too small for him, before he slept. "And I fear it shall come to us with barbecue sauce."

*

They were all so hungry the following morning. Zebediah T. Crawcrustle had a comedic apron on, with the words KISS THE COOK written upon it in violently green letters. He had already sprinkled the brandy-soaked raisins and grain beneath the stunted avocado tree behind the house, and he was arranging the scented woods, the herbs, and the spices on the bed of charcoal. Mustapha Stroheim and his family had gone to visit relatives on the other side of Cairo.

"Does anybody have a match?" Crawcrustle asked.

Jackie Newhouse pulled out a Zippo lighter, and passed it to Crawcrustle, who lit the dried cinnamon leaves and dried laurel leaves beneath the charcoal. The smoke drifted up into the noon air.

"The cinnamon and sandalwood smoke will bring the Sunbird," said Crawcrustle.

"Bring it from where?" asked Augustus TwoFeathers McCoy.

"From the Sun," said Crawcrustle. "That's where he sleeps."

Professor Mandalay coughed discreetly. He said, "The Earth is, at its closest, ninety-one million miles from the Sun. The fastest dive by a bird ever recorded is that of the peregrine falcon, at two hundred and seventy-three miles per hour. Flying at that speed, from the Sun, it would take a bird a little over thirty-eight years to reach us—if it could fly through the dark and cold and vacuum of space, of course."

"Of course," agreed Zebediah T. Crawcrustle. He shaded his eyes and squinted and looked upward. "Here it comes," he said.

It looked almost as if the bird was flying out of the sun; but that could not have been the case. You could not look directly at the noonday sun, after all.

First it was a silhouette, black against the sun and against the blue sky, then the sunlight caught its feathers, and the watchers on the ground caught their breath. You have never seen anything like sunlight on the Sunbird's feathers; seeing something like that would take your breath away.

The Sunbird flapped its wide wings once, then it began to glide in ever-decreasing circles in the air above Mustapha Stroheim's coffeehouse.

The bird landed in the avocado tree. Its feathers were golden, and purple, and silver. It was smaller than a turkey, larger than a rooster, and had the long legs and high head of a heron, though its head was more like the head of an eagle.

"It is very beautiful," said Virginia Boote. "Look at the two tall feathers on its head. Aren't they lovely?"

"It is indeed quite lovely," said Professor Mandalay.

"There is something familiar about that bird's headfeathers," said Augustus TwoFeathers McCoy.

"We pluck the headfeathers before we roast the bird," said Zebediah T. Crawcrustle. "It's the way it's always done."

The Sunbird perched on a branch of the avocado tree, in a patch of sun. It seemed almost as if it were glowing, gently, in the sunlight, as if its feathers were made of sunlight, iridescent with purples and greens and golds. It preened itself, extending one wing in the sunlight. It nibbled and stroked at the wing with its beak until all the feathers were in their correct position, and oiled. Then it extended the other wing, and repeated the process. Finally, the bird emitted a contented chirrup, and flew the short distance from the branch to the ground.

It strutted across the dried mud, peering from side to side shortsightedly.

"Look!" said Jackie Newhouse. "It's found the grain."

"It seemed almost that it was looking for it," said Augustus TwoFeathers McCoy. "That it was expecting the grain to be there."

"That's where I always leave it," said Zebediah T. Crawcrustle.

"It's so lovely," said Virginia Boote. "But now I see it closer, I can see that it's much older than I thought. Its eyes are cloudy and its legs are shaking. But it's still lovely."

"The Bennu bird is the loveliest of birds," said Zebediah T. Crawcrustle.

Virginia Boote spoke good restaurant Egyptian, but beyond that she was all at sea. "What's a Bennu bird?" she asked. "Is that Egyptian for Sunbird?"

"The Bennu bird," said Professor Mandalay, "roosts in the Persea tree. It has two feathers on its head. It is sometimes represented as being like a heron, and sometimes like an eagle. There is more, but it is too unlikely to bear repeating."

"It's eaten the grain and the raisins!" exclaimed Jackie Newhouse. "Now it's stumbling drunkenly from side to side—such majesty, even in its drunkenness!"

Zebediah T. Crawcrustle walked over to the

Sunbird, which, with a great effort of will, was staggering back and forth on the mud beneath the avocado tree, not tripping over its long legs. He stood directly in front of the bird, and then, very slowly, he bowed to it. He bent like an extremely old man, slowly and creakily, but still he bowed. And the Sunbird bowed back to him, then it toppled to the mud. Zebediah T. Crawcrustle picked it up reverently, and placed it in his arms, carrying it as one would carry a child, and he took it back to the plot of land behind Mustapha Stroheim's coffeehouse, and the others followed him.

First he plucked the two majestic headfeathers, and set them aside.

And then, without plucking the bird, he gutted it, and placed the guts on the smoking twigs. He put the half-filled beer can inside the body cavity, and placed the bird upon the barbecue.

"Sunbird cooks fast," warned Crawcrustle. "Get your plates ready."

The beers of the ancient Egyptians were flavored with cardamom and coriander, for the Egyptians had no hops; their beers were rich and flavorsome and thirst quenching. You could build pyramids after drinking that beer, and sometimes people did. On the barbecue the beer steamed the inside of the Sunbird, keeping it moist. As the heat of the charcoal reached them, the feathers of the bird burned off, igniting with a flash like a magnesium flare, so bright that the Epicureans were forced to avert their eyes.

The smell of roast fowl filled the air, richer than peacock, lusher than duck. The mouths of the assembled Epicureans began to water. It seemed like it had been cooking for no time at all, but Zebediah lifted the Sunbird from the charcoal bed and put it on the table. Then, with a carving knife, he sliced it up and placed the steaming meat on the plates. He poured a little barbecue sauce over each piece of meat. He placed the carcass directly onto the flames.

Each member of the Epicurean Club sat in the back of Mustapha Stroheim's coffeehouse, sat around an elderly wooden table, and they ate with their fingers.

"Zebby, this is amazing!" said Virginia Boote, talking as she ate. "It melts in your mouth. It tastes like heaven."

"It tastes like the sun," said Augustus TwoFeathers

McCoy, putting his food away as only a big man can. He had a leg in one hand, and some breast in the other. "It is the finest thing I have ever eaten, and I do not regret eating it, but I do believe that I shall miss my daughter."

"It is perfect," said Jackie Newhouse. "It tastes like love and fine music. It tastes like truth."

Professor Mandalay was scribbling in the bound annals of the Epicurean Club. He was recording his reaction to the meat of the bird, and recording the reactions of the other Epicureans, and trying not to drip on the page while he wrote, for with the hand that was not writing he was holding a wing, and, fastidiously, he was nibbling the meat off it.

"It is strange," said Jackie Newhouse, "for as I eat it, it gets hotter and hotter in my mouth and in my stomach."

"Yup. It'll do that. It's best to prepare for it ahead of time," said Zebediah T. Crawcrustle. "Eat coals and flames and lightning bugs to get used to it. Otherwise it can be a trifle hard on the system."

Zebediah T. Crawcrustle was eating the head of the bird, crunching its bones and beak in his mouth. As he ate, the bones sparked small lightnings against his teeth. He just grinned and chewed the more.

The bones of the Sunbird's carcass burned orange on the barbecue, and then they began to burn white. There was a thick heat haze in the courtyard at the back of Mustapha Stroheim's coffeehouse, and in it everything shimmered, as if the people around the table were seeing the world through water or a dream.

"It is so good!" said Virginia Boote as she ate. "It is the best thing I have ever eaten. It tastes like my youth. It tastes like forever." She licked her fingers, then picked up the last slice of meat from her plate. "The Sunbird of Suntown," she said. "Does it have another name?"

"It is the Phoenix of Heliopolis," said Zebediah T. Crawcrustle. "It is the bird that dies in ashes and flame, and is born again, generation after generation. It is the Bennu bird, which flew across the waters when all was dark. When its time is come it is burned on the fire of rare woods and spices and herbs, and in the ashes it is reborn, time after time, world without end."

"Fire!" exclaimed Professor Mandalay. "It feels as if my insides are burning up!" He sipped his water, but seemed no happier.

"My fingers," said Virginia Boote. "Look at my fingers." She held them up. They were glowing inside, as if lit with inner flames.

Now the air was so hot you could have baked an egg in it.

There was a spark and a sputter. The two yellow feathers in Augustus TwoFeathers McCoy's hair went up like sparklers. "Crawcrustle," said Jackie Newhouse, aflame, "answer me truly. How long have you been eating the Phoenix?"

"A little over ten thousand years," said Zebediah. "Give or take a few thousand. It's not hard, once you master the trick of it; it's just mastering the trick of it that's hard. But this is the best Phoenix I've ever prepared. Or do I mean, 'This is the best I've ever cooked this Phoenix'?"

"The years!" said Virginia Boote. "They are burning off you!"

"They do that," admitted Zebediah. "You've got to get used to the heat, though, before you eat it. Otherwise you can just burn away."

"Why did I not remember this?" said Augustus TwoFeathers McCoy, through the bright flames that surrounded him. "Why did I not remember that this was how my father went, and his father before him, that each of them went to Heliopolis to eat the Phoenix? And why do I only remember it now?"

"Because the years are burning off you," said Professor Mandalay. He had closed the leather book as soon as the page he had been writing on caught fire. The edges of the book were charred, but the rest of the book would be fine. "When the years burn, the memories of those years come back." He looked more solid now, through the wavering burning air, and he was smiling. None of them had ever seen Professor Mandalay smile before.

"Shall we burn away to nothing?" asked Virginia, now incandescent. "Or shall we burn back to childhood and burn back to ghosts and angels and then come forward again? It does not matter. Oh Crusty, this is all such *fun!*"

"Perhaps," said Jackie Newhouse, through the fire, "there might have been a little more vinegar in the sauce. I feel a meat like this could have dealt with something more robust." And then he was gone, leaving only an afterimage.

"*Chacun à son goût,*" said Zebediah T.

Crawcrustle, which is French for "each to his own taste," and he licked his fingers and he shook his head. "Best it's ever been," he said, with enormous satisfaction.

"Good-bye, Crusty," said Virginia. She put her flame-white hand out, and held his dark hand tightly for one moment, or perhaps for two.

And then there was nothing in the courtyard back of Mustapha Stroheim's *kahwa* (or coffeehouse) in Heliopolis (which was once the city of the Sun, and is now a suburb of Cairo) but white ash, which blew up in the momentary breeze, and settled like powdered sugar or like snow; and nobody there but a young man with dark, dark hair and even, ivory-colored teeth, wearing an apron that said KISS THE COOK.

A tiny golden-purple bird stirred in the thick bed of ashes on top of the clay bricks, as if it were waking for the first time. It made a high-pitched *peep!* and it looked directly into the sun, as an infant looks at a parent. It stretched its wings as if to dry them, and, eventually, when it was quite ready, it flew upward, toward the sun, and nobody watched it leave but the young man in the courtyard.

There were two long golden feathers at the young man's feet, beneath the ash that had once been a wooden table, and he gathered them up, and brushed the white ash from them and placed them, reverently, inside his jacket. Then he removed his apron, and he went upon his way.

Hollyberry TwoFeathers McCoy is a grown woman, with children of her own. There are silver hairs on her head, in there with the black, beneath the golden feathers in the bun at the back. You can see that once the feathers must have looked pretty special, but that would have been a long time ago. She is the president of the Epicurean Club—a rich and rowdy bunch—having inherited the position, many long years ago, from her father.

I hear that the Epicureans are beginning to grumble once again. They are saying that they have eaten everything.

(For HMG—a belated birthday present)

The Witch's Headstone

THERE WAS A WITCH buried at the edge of the graveyard; it was common knowledge. Bod had been told to keep away from that corner of the world by Mrs. Owens as far back as he could remember.

"Why?" he asked.

"'Tain't healthy for a living body," said Mrs. Owens. "There's damp down that end of things. It's practically a marsh. You'll catch your death."

Mr. Owens himself was more evasive and less imaginative. "It's not a good place" was all he said.

The graveyard proper ended at the bottom of the hill, beneath the old apple tree, with a fence of rust-brown iron railings, each topped with a small, rusting spearhead, but there was a wasteland beyond that, a mass of nettles and weeds, of brambles and autumnal rubbish, and Bod, who was a good boy, on the whole, and obedient, did not push between the railings, but he went down there and looked through. He knew he wasn't being told the whole story, and it irritated him.

Bod went back up the hill, to the abandoned church in the middle of the graveyard, and he waited until it got dark. As twilight edged from gray to purple there was a noise in the spire, like a fluttering of heavy velvet, and Silas left his resting place in the belfry and clambered headfirst down the spire.

"What's in the far corner of the graveyard," asked Bod. "Past Harrison Westwood, Baker of this Parish, and his wives, Marion and Joan?"

"Why do you ask?" said his guardian, brushing the dust from his black suit with ivory fingers.

Bod shrugged. "Just wondered."

"It's unconsecrated ground," said Silas. "Do you know what that means?"

"Not really," said Bod.

Silas walked across the path without disturbing a fallen leaf, and sat down on the stone bench, beside Bod. "There are those," he said in his silken voice, "who believe that all land is sacred. That it is sacred before we come to it, and sacred after. But here, in your land, they bless the churches and the ground

they set aside to bury people in, to make it holy. But they leave land unconsecrated beside the sacred ground, potter's fields to bury the criminals and the suicides or those who were not of the faith."

"So the people buried in the ground on the other side of the fence are bad people?"

Silas raised one perfect eyebrow. "Mm? Oh, not at all. Let's see, it's been a while since I've been down that way. But I don't remember anyone particularly evil. Remember, in days gone by you could be hanged for stealing a shilling. And there are always people who find their lives have become so unsupportable they believe the best thing they could do would be to hasten their transition to another plane of existence."

"They kill themselves, you mean?" said Bod. He was about eight years old, wide-eyed and inquisitive, and he was not stupid.

"Indeed."

"Does it work? Are they happier dead?"

Silas grinned so wide and sudden that he showed his fangs. "Sometimes. Mostly, no. It's like the people who believe they'll be happy if they go and live somewhere else, but who learn it doesn't work that way. Wherever you go, you take yourself with you. If you see what I mean."

"Sort of," said Bod.

Silas reached down and ruffled the boy's hair.

Bod said, "What about the witch?"

"Yes. Exactly," said Silas. "Suicides, criminals, and witches. Those who died unshriven." He stood up, a midnight shadow in the twilight. "All this talking," he said, "and I have not even had my breakfast. While you will be late for lessons." In the twilight of the graveyard there was a silent implosion, a flutter of velvet darkness, and Silas was gone.

The moon had begun to rise by the time Bod reached Mr. Pennyworth's mausoleum, and Thomes Pennyworth (*here he lyes in the certainty of the moft glorious refurrection*) was already waiting, and was not in the best of moods.

"You are late," he said.

"Sorry, Mr. Pennyworth."

Pennyworth tutted. The previous week Mr. Pennyworth had been teaching Bod about Elements and Humors, and Bod had kept forgetting which was which. He was expecting a test, but instead Mr. Pennyworth said, "I think it is time to spend a few days on practical matters. Time is passing, after all."

"Is it?" asked Bod.

"I am afraid so, young Master Owens. Now, how is your Fading?"

Bod had hoped he would not be asked that question.

"It's all right," he said. "I mean. You know."

"No, Master Owens. I do not know. Why do you not demonstrate for me?"

Bod's heart sank. He took a deep breath, and did his best, squinching up his eyes and trying to fade away.

Mr. Pennyworth was not impressed.

"Pah. That's not the kind of thing. Not the kind of thing at all. Slipping and fading, boy, the way of the dead. Slip through shadows. Fade from awareness. Try again."

Bod tried harder.

"You're as plain as the nose on your face," said Mr. Pennyworth. "And your nose is remarkably obvious. As is the rest of your face, young man. As are you. For the sake of all that is holy, empty your mind. Now. You are an empty alleyway. You are a vacant doorway. You are nothing. Eyes will not see you.

Minds will not hold you. Where you are is nothing and nobody."

Bod tried again. He closed his eyes and imagined himself fading into the stained stonework of the mausoleum wall, becoming a shadow on the night and nothing more. He sneezed.

"Dreadful," said Mr. Pennyworth with a sigh. "Quite dreadful. I believe I shall have a word with your guardian about this." He shook his head. "So. The humors. List them."

"Um. Sanguine. Choleric. Phlegmatic. And the other one. Um, Melancholic, I think."

And so it went, until it was time for Grammar and Composition with Miss Letitia Borrows, Spinster of this Parish (*Who Did No Harm to No Man all the Dais of Her Life. Reader, Can You Say Lykewise?*). Bod liked Miss Borrows, and the coziness of her little crypt, and that she could all too easily be led off the subject.

"They say there's a witch in the uncons—unconsecrated ground," he said.

"Yes, dear. But you don't want to go over there."

"Why not?"

Miss Borrows smiled the guileless smile of the

dead. "They aren't our sort of people," she said.

"But it *is* the graveyard, isn't it? I mean, I'm allowed to go there if I want to?"

"That," said Miss Borrows, "would not be advisable."

Bod was obedient but curious, and so, when lessons were done for the night, he walked past Harrison Westwood, Baker, and family's memorial, a broken-headed angel, but did not climb down the hill to the potter's field. Instead he walked up the side of the hill to where a picnic some thirty years before had left its mark in the shape of a large apple tree.

There were some lessons that Bod had mastered. He had eaten a bellyful of unripe apples, sour and white-pipped, from the tree some years before, and had regretted it for days, his guts cramping and painful while Mrs. Owens lectured him on what not to eat. Now he waited until the apples were ripe before eating them, and never ate more than two or three a night. He had finished the last of the apples the week before, but he liked the apple tree as a place to think.

He edged up the trunk, to his favorite place in the

crook of two branches, and looked down at the pot-ter's field below him, a brambly patch of weeds and unmown grass in the moonlight. He wondered whether the witch would be old and iron-toothed and travel in a house on chicken legs, or whether she would be thin and sharp-nosed and carry a broom-stick.

And then he was hungry. He wished he had not devoured all the apples on the tree. That he had left just one . . .

He glanced up, and thought he saw something. He looked once, looked twice to be certain. An apple, red and ripe.

Bod prided himself on his tree-climbing skills. He swung himself up, branch by branch, and imagined he was Silas swarming smoothly up a sheer brick wall. The apple, the red of it almost black in the moonlight, hung just out of reach. Bod moved slowly forward along the branch, until he was just below the apple. Then he stretched up, and the tips of his fingers touched the perfect apple.

He was never to taste it.

A snap, loud as a hunter's gun, as the branch gave way beneath him.

*

A flash of pain woke him, sharp as ice, the color of slow thunder, down in the weeds that summer's night.

The ground beneath him seemed relatively soft, and oddly warm. He pushed a hand down and felt something like warm fur beneath him. He had landed on the grass pile, where the graveyard's gardener threw the cuttings from the mower, and it had broken his fall. Still, there was a pain in his chest, and his leg hurt as if he had landed on it first and twisted it.

Bod moaned.

"Hush-a-you-hush-a-boy," said a voice from behind him. "Where did you come from? Dropping like a thunderstone. What way is that to carry on?"

"I was in the apple tree," said Bod.

"Ah. Let me see your leg. Broken like the tree's limb, I'll be bound." Cool fingers prodded his left leg. "Not broken. Twisted, yes, sprained perhaps. You have the Devil's own luck, boy, falling into the compost. 'Tain't the end of the world."

"Oh, good," said Bod. "Hurts, though."

He turned his head, looked up and behind him.

She was older than him but not a grown-up, and she looked neither friendly nor unfriendly. Wary, mostly. She had a face that was intelligent and not even a little bit beautiful.

"I'm Bod," he said.

"The live boy?" she asked.

Bod nodded.

"I thought you must be," she said. "We've heard of you, even over here, in the potter's field. What do they call you?"

"Owens," he said. "Nobody Owens. Bod, for short."

"How-de-do, young Master Bod."

Bod looked her up and down. She wore a plain white shift. Her hair was mousy and long, and there was something of the goblin in her face—a sideways hint of a smile that seemed to linger, no matter what the rest of her face was doing.

"Were you a suicide?" he asked. "Did you steal a shilling?"

"Never stole nuffink," she said, "not even a handkerchief. Anyway," she said pertly, "the suicides is all over there, on the other side of that hawthorn, and the gallows birds are in the blackberry patch, both of

213

them. One was a coiner, t'other a highwayman, or so he says, although if you ask me I doubt he was more than a common footpad and nightwalker."

"Ah," said Bod. Then, suspicion forming, tentatively, he said, "They say a witch is buried here."

She nodded. "Drownded and burnded and buried here without as much as a stone to mark the spot."

"You were drowned *and* burned?"

She settled down on the hill of grass cuttings beside him, and held his throbbing leg with her chilly hands. "They come to my little cottage at dawn, before I'm proper awake, and drags me out onto the green. 'You're a witch!' they shouts, fat and fresh-scrubbed all pink in the morning, like so many pigwiggins scrubbed clean for market day. One by one they gets up beneath the sky and tells of milk gone sour and horses gone lame, and finally Mistress Jemima gets up, the fattest, pinkest, best scrubbed of them all, and tells how as Solomon Porritt now cuts her dead and instead hangs around the washhouse like a wasp about a honeypot, and it's all my magic, says she, that made him so and the poor young man must be bespelled. So they strap me to the cucking stool and forces it under the water of the duck pond, saying if I'm a witch I'll neither drown nor care, but if I am not a witch I'll feel it. And Mistress Jemima's father gives them each a silver groat to hold the stool down under the foul green water for a long time, to see if I'd choke on it."

"And did you?"

"Oh yes. Got a lungful of water. It done for me."

"Oh," said Bod. "Then you weren't a witch after all."

The girl fixed him with her beady ghost eyes and smiled a lopsided smile. She still looked like a goblin, but now she looked like a pretty goblin, and Bod didn't think she would have needed magic to attract Solomon Porritt, not with a smile like that. "What nonsense. Of course I was a witch. They learned that when they untied me from the cucking stool and stretched me on the green, nine parts dead and all covered with duckweed and stinking pond muck. I rolled my eyes back in my head, and I cursed each and every one of them there on the village green that morning, that none of them would ever rest easily in a grave. I was surprised at how easily it came, the cursing. Like dancing it was, when your feet pick up the steps of a new measure your ears have never heard and your head don't know, and they dance it till dawn." She stood, and twirled, and kicked, and her bare feet flashed in the moonlight. "That was how I cursed them, with my last gurgling pond-watery breath. And then I expired. They burned my body on the green until I was nothing but blackened charcoal, and they popped me in a hole in the potter's field without so much as a head-stone to mark my name," and it was only then that she paused, and seemed, for a moment, wistful.

"Are any of them buried in the graveyard, then?" asked Bod.

"Not a one," said the girl, with a twinkle. "The Saturday after they drownded and toasted me, a carpet was delivered to Master Porringer, all the way from London Town, and it was a fine carpet. But it turned out there was more in that carpet than strong wool and good weaving, for it carried the plague in its pattern, and by Monday five of them were coughing blood, and their skins were gone as black as mine when they hauled me from the fire. A week later and it had taken most of the village, and they threw the bodies all promiscuous in a plague pit they dug outside of the town, that they filled in after."

"Was everyone in the village killed?"

She shrugged. "Everyone who watched me get drownded and burned. How's your leg now?"

"Better," he said. "Thanks."

Bod stood up slowly, and limped down from the grass pile. He leaned against the iron railings. "So were you always a witch?" he asked. "I mean, before you cursed them all?"

"As if it would take witchcraft," she said with a sniff, "to get Solomon Porritt mooning 'round my cottage."

Which, Bod thought, but did not say, was not actually an answer to the question, not at all.

"What's your name?" he asked.

"Got no headstone," she said, turning down the corners of her mouth. "Might be anybody. Mightn't I?"

"But you must have a name."

"Liza Hempstock, if you please," she said tartly. Then she said, "It's not that much to ask, is it? Something to mark my grave. I'm just down there, see? With nothing but nettles to show where I rest." And she looked so sad, just for a moment, that Bod wanted to hug her. And then it came to him, and as he squeezed between the railings of the fence. He would find Liza Hempstock a headstone, with her name upon it. He would make her smile.

He turned to wave good-bye as he began to clamber up the hill, but she was already gone.

There were broken lumps of other people's stones and statues in the graveyard, but, Bod knew, that would have been entirely the wrong sort of thing to bring to the gray-eyed witch in the potter's field. It was going to take more than that. He decided not to tell anyone what he was planning, on the not entirely unreasonable basis that they would have told him not to do it.

Over the next few days his mind filled with plans, each more complicated and extravagant than the last. Mr. Pennyworth despaired.

"I do believe," he announced, scratching his dusty mustache, "that you are getting, if anything, worse. You are not Fading. You are *obvious*, boy. You are difficult to miss. If you came to me in company with a purple lion, a green elephant, and a scarlet unicorn astride which was the King of England in his royal robes, I do believe that it is you and you alone that people would stare at, dismissing the others as minor irrelevancies."

Bod simply stared at him, and said nothing. He was wondering whether there were special shops in the places where the living people gathered that sold only headstones, and if so how he could go about finding one, and Fading was the least of his problems.

He took advantage of Miss Borrow's willingness to be diverted from the subjects of grammar and composition to the subject of anything else at all to ask her about money—how exactly it worked, how one used it to get things one wanted. Bod had a number of coins he had found over the years (he had learned that the best place to find money was to go, afterward, to wherever courting couples had used the grass of the graveyard as a place to cuddle and snuggle and kiss and roll about. He would often find metal coins on the ground, in the place where they had been), and he thought perhaps he could finally get some use from them.

"How much would a headstone be?" he asked Miss Borrows.

"In my time," she told him, "they were fifteen guineas. I do not know what they would be today. More, I imagine. Much, much more."

Bod had fifty-three pence. It would, he was quite certain, not be enough.

It had been four years, almost half a lifetime, since Bod had visited the Indigo Man's tomb. But he still remembered the way. He climbed to the top of the hill, until he was above the whole town, above even the top of the apple tree, above even the steeple of the ruined church, up where the Frobisher vault stood like a rotten tooth. He slipped down into it, and down and down and still farther down, down to the tiny stone steps cut into the center of the hill, and those he descended until he reached the stone chamber at the base of the hill. It was dark in that tomb, dark as a deep mine, but Bod saw as the dead see and the room gave up its secrets to him.

The Sleer was coiled around the wall of the barrow. It was as he remembered it, all smoky tendrils and hate and greed. This time, however, he was not afraid of it.

FEAR ME, whispered the Sleer. FOR I GUARD THINGS PRECIOUS AND NEVER-LOST.

"I don't fear you," said Bod. "Remember? And I need to take something away from here."

Nothing ever leaves, came the reply from the coiled thing in the darkness. The Knife, the Brooch, the Goblet. I guard them in the darkness. I wait.

In the center of the room was a slab of rock, and on it they lay: a stone knife, a brooch, and a goblet.

"Pardon me for asking," said Bod, "but was this your grave?"

Master sets us here on the plain to guard, buries our skulls beneath this stone, leaves us here knowing what we have to do. We guards the treasures until Master comes back.

"I expect that he's forgotten all about you," pointed out Bod. "I'm sure he's been dead himself for ages."

We are the Sleer. We guard.

Bod wondered just how long ago you had to go back before the deepest tomb inside the hill was on a plain, and he knew it must have been an extremely long time ago. He could feel the Sleer winding its waves of fear around him, like the tendrils of some carnivorous plant. He was beginning to feel cold, and slow, as if he had been bitten in the heart by some arctic viper and it was starting to pump its icy venom through his body.

He took a step forward, so he was standing against the stone slab, and he reached down and closed his fingers around the coldness of the brooch.

HISH! whispered the Sleer. WE GUARDS THAT FOR THE MASTER.

"He won't mind," said Bod. He took a step backward, walking toward the stone steps, avoiding the desiccated remains of people and animals on the floor.

The Sleer writhed angrily, twining around the tiny chamber like ghost smoke. Then it slowed. IT COMES BACK, said the Sleer in its tangled triple voice. ALWAYS COMES BACK.

Bod went up the stone steps inside the hill as fast as he could. At one point he imagined that there was something coming after him, but when he broke out of the top, into the Frobisher vault, and he could breathe the cool dawn air, nothing moved or followed.

Bod sat in the open air on the top of the hill and held the brooch. He thought it was all black, at first, but then the sun rose, and he could see that the stone in the center of the black metal was a swirling red. It was the size of a robin's egg, and Bod stared into the stone wondering if there were things moving in its heart, his eyes and soul deep in the crimson world. If Bod had been smaller he would have wanted to put it into his mouth.

The stone was held in place by a black metal clasp, by something that looked like claws, with something else crawling around it. The something else looked almost snakelike, but it had too many heads. Bod wondered if that was what the Sleer looked like, in the daylight.

He wandered down the hill, taking all the shortcuts he knew, through the ivy tangle that covered the Bartleby family vault (and inside, the sound of the Bartlebies grumbling and readying for sleep) and on and over and through the railings and into the potter's field.

He called, "Liza! Liza!" and looked around.

"Good morrow, young lummox," said Liza's voice. Bod could not see her, but there was an extra shadow beneath the hawthorn tree, and, as he approached it, the shadow resolved itself into something pearlescent and translucent in the early-morning light. Something girl-like. Something gray eyed. "I should be decently sleeping," she said. "What kind of carrying-on is this?"

"Your headstone," he said. "I wanted to know what you want on it."

"My name," she said. "It must have my name on it, with a big E, for Elizabeth, like the old queen that died when I was born, and a big haitch, for Hempstock. More than that I care not, for I did never master my letters."

"What about dates?" asked Bod.

"Willyum the Conker ten sixty-six," she sang, in the whisper of the dawn wind in the hawthorn bush. "A big E if you please. And a big haitch."

"Did you have a job?" asked Bod. "I mean, when you weren't being a witch?"

"I done laundry," said the dead girl, and then the morning sunlight flooded the wasteland, and Bod was alone.

It was nine in the morning, when all the world is sleeping. Bod was determined to stay awake. He was, after all, on a mission. He was eight years old, and the world beyond the graveyard held no terrors for him.

Clothes. He would need clothes. His usual dress, of a gray winding sheet, was, he knew, quite wrong. It was good in the graveyard, the same color as stone and as shadows. But if he was going to dare the world beyond the graveyard walls, he would need to blend in there.

There were some clothes in the crypt beneath the ruined church, but Bod did not want to go down to the crypt, not even in daylight. While Bod was prepared to justify himself to Master and Mistress Owens, he was not about to explain himself to Silas; the very thought of those dark eyes angry, or worse still, disappointed, filled him with shame.

There was a gardener's hut at the far end of the graveyard, a small green building that smelled like motor oil and in which the old mower sat and rusted, unused, along with an assortment of ancient garden tools. The hut had been abandoned when the last gardener had retired, before Bod was born, and the task of keeping the graveyard had been shared between the council (who sent in a man to cut the grass, once a month from April to September) and local volunteers.

A huge padlock on the door protected the contents of the hut, but Bod had long ago discovered the loose wooden board in the back. Sometimes he would go to the gardener's hut, and sit, and think, when he wanted to be by himself.

As long as he had been going to the hut there had been a brown workingman's jacket hanging on the back of the door, forgotten or abandoned years before, along with a green-stained pair of gardening jeans. The jeans were much too big for him, but he rolled up the cuffs until his feet showed, then he made a belt out of brown garden twine, and tied it around his waist. There were boots in one corner, and he tried putting them on, but they were so big and encrusted with mud and concrete that he could barely shuffle them, and if he took a step, the boots remained on the floor of the shed. He pushed the jacket out through the space in the loose board, squeezed himself out, then put it on. If he rolled up the sleeves, he decided, it worked quite well. It had big pockets, and he thrust his hands into them, and felt quite the dandy.

Bod walked down to the main gate of the graveyard, and looked out through the bars. A bus rattled past in the street; there were cars there and noise and shops. Behind him, a cool green shade, overgrown with trees and ivy: home.

His heart pounding, Bod walked out into the world.

Abanazer Bolger had seen some odd types in his time; if you owned a shop like Abanazer's, you'd see them too. The shop, in the warren of streets in the Old Town—a little bit antique shop, a little bit junk shop, a little bit pawnbroker's (and not even Abanazer himself was entirely certain which bit was which)—brought odd types and strange people, some of them wanting to buy, some of them needing to sell. Abanazer Bolger traded over the counter, buying and selling, and he did a better trade behind the counter and in the back room, accepting objects that may not have been acquired entirely honestly, and then quietly shifting them on. His business was an iceberg. Only the dusty little shop was visible on the surface. The rest of it was underneath, and that was just how Abanazer Bolger wanted it.

Abanazer Bolger had thick spectacles and a permanent expression of mild distaste, as if he had just realized that the milk in his tea had been on the turn and he could not get the sour taste of it out of his mouth. The expression served him well when people tried to sell him things. "Honestly," he would tell them, sour faced, "it's not really worth anything at all. I'll give you what I can, though, as it has sentimental value." You were lucky to get anything like what you thought you wanted from Abanazer Bolger.

A business like Abanazer Bolger's brought in strange people, but the boy who came in that morning was one of the strangest Abanazer could remember in a lifetime of cheating strange people out of their valuables. He looked to be about seven years old, and dressed in his grandfather's clothes. He smelled like a shed. His feet were bare. His hair was long and shaggy, and he looked extremely grave. His hands were deep in the pockets of a dusty brown jacket, but even with the hands out of sight, Abanazer could see that something was clutched extremely tightly—protectively—in the boy's right hand.

"Excuse me," said the boy.

"Aye, aye, Sonny Jim," said Abanazer Bolger warily.

Kids, he thought. *They've nicked something, or they're trying to sell their toys.* Whichever it was, he usually said no. Buy stolen property from a kid, and next thing you knew you'd have an enraged adult accusing you of having given little Johnnie or Matilda a tenner for their wedding ring. More trouble than they was worth, kids.

"I need something for a friend of mine," said the boy. "And I thought maybe you could buy something I've got."

"I don't buy stuff from kids," said Abanazer Bolger flatly.

Bod took his hand out of his pocket and put the brooch down on the grimy counter top. Bolger glanced at it, then he looked at it. He removed his spectacles. He took an eyepiece from the counter top and he screwed it into his eye. He turned on a little light on the counter and examined the brooch through the eyeglass. "Snakestone?" he said, to himself, not to the boy. Then he took the eyepiece out, replaced his glasses, and fixed the boy with a sour and suspicious look.

"Where did you get this?" Abanazer Bolger asked.

Bod said, "Do you want to buy it?"

"You stole it. You've nicked this from a museum or somewhere, didn't you?"

"No," said Bod flatly. "Are you going to buy it, or shall I go and find somebody who will?"

Abanazer Bolger's sour mood changed then. Suddenly he was all affability. He smiled broadly. "I'm sorry," he said. "It's just you don't see many pieces like this. Not in a shop like this. Not outside of a museum. But I would certainly like it. Tell you what. Why don't we sit down over tea and biscuits—I've got a packet of chocolate chip cookies in the back room—and decide how much something like this is worth? Eh?"

Bod was relieved that the man was finally being friendly. "I need enough to buy a stone," he said. "A headstone for a friend of mine. Well, she's not really my friend. Just someone I know. I think she helped make my leg better, you see."

Abanazer Bolger, paying little attention to the boy's prattle, led him behind the counter, and opened the door to the storeroom, a windowless little space every inch of which was crammed high with teetering cardboard boxes, each filled with junk. There was a safe in there, in the corner, a big old one. There was a box filled with violins, an accumulation of stuffed dead animals, chairs without seats, books and prints.

There was a small desk beside the door, and Abanazer Bolger pulled up the only chair, and sat down, letting Bod stand. Abanazer rummaged in a drawer, in which Bod could see a half-empty bottle of whiskey, and pulled out an almost-finished packet of chocolate chip cookies, and he offered one to the boy; he turned on the desk light, looked at the brooch again, the swirls of red and orange in the stone, and he examined the black metal band that encircled it, suppressing a little shiver at the expression on the heads of the snake things. "This is old," he said. "It's—" *priceless*, he thought, "—probably not really worth much, but you never know." Bod's face fell. Abanazer Bolger tried to look reassuring. "I just need to be sure that it's not stolen, though, before I can give you a penny. Did you take it from your mum's dresser? Nick it from a museum? You can tell me. I'll not get you into trouble. I just need to know."

Bod shook his head. He munched on his cookie.

"Then where did you get it?"

Bod said nothing.

Abanazer Bolger did not want to put down the brooch, but he pushed it across the desk to the boy. "If you can't tell me," he said, "you'd better take it back. There has to be trust on both sides, after all. Nice doing business with you. Sorry it couldn't go any further."

Bod looked worried. Then he said, "I found it in an old grave. But I can't say where." And then he stopped, because naked greed and excitement had replaced the friendliness on Abanazer Bolger's face.

"And there's more like this there?"

Bod said, "If you don't want to buy it, I'll find someone else. Thank you for the biscuit."

Bolger said, "You're in a hurry, eh? Mum and Dad waiting for you, I expect?"

The boy shook his head, then wished he had nodded.

"Nobody waiting. Good." Abanazer Bolger closed his hands around the brooch. "Now, you tell me exactly where you found this. Eh?"

"I don't remember," said Bod.

"Too late for that," said Abanazer Bolger. "Suppose you have a serious think for a bit about where it came from. Then, when you've thought, we'll have a little chat, and you'll tell me."

He got up, and walked out of the room, closing the door behind him. He locked it, with a large metal key.

He opened his hand, and looked at the brooch and smiled, hungrily.

There was a *ding* from the bell above the shop door, to let him know someone had entered, and he looked up guiltily, but there was nobody there. The door was slightly ajar though, so Bolger pushed it shut, and then for good measure, he turned around the sign in the window, so it said CLOSED. He pushed the bolt shut. Didn't want any busybodies turning up today.

The autumn day had turned from sunny to gray, and a light patter of rain ran down the grubby shop window.

Abanazer Bolger picked up the telephone from the counter and pushed at the buttons with fingers that barely shook.

"Paydirt, Tom," he said. "Get over here, soon as you can."

Bod realized that he was trapped when he heard the

lock turn in the door. He pulled on the door, but it held fast. He felt stupid for having been lured inside, foolish for not trusting his first impulses to get as far away from the sour-faced man as possible. He had broken all the rules of the graveyard, and everything had gone wrong. What would Silas say? Or the Owens? He could feel himself beginning to panic, and he suppressed it, pushing the worry back down inside him. It would all be good. He knew that. Of course, he needed to get out. . . .

He examined the room he was trapped in. It was little more than a storeroom with a desk in it. The only entrance was the door.

He opened the desk drawer, finding nothing but small pots of paint (used for brightening up antiques) and a paintbrush. He wondered if he would be able to throw paint in the man's face and blind him for long enough to escape. He opened the top of a pot of paint and dipped in his finger.

"What're you doin'?" asked a voice close to his ear.

"Nothing," said Bod, screwing the top on the paintpot and dropping it into one of the jacket's enormous pockets.

Liza Hempstock looked at him, unimpressed.

"Why are you in here?" she asked. "And who's the old bag of lard out there?"

"It's his shop. I was trying to sell him something."

"Why?"

"None of your beeswax."

She sniffed. "Well," she said, "you should get on back to the graveyard."

"I can't. He's locked me in."

"Course you can. Just slip through the wall—"

He shook his head. "I can't. I can only do it at home because they gave me the freedom of the graveyard when I was a baby." He looked up at her, under the electric light. It was hard to see her properly, but Bod had spent his life talking to dead people. "Anyway, what are you doing here? What are you doing out from the graveyard? It's daytime. And you're not like Silas. You're meant to stay in the graveyard."

She said, "There's rules for those in graveyards, but not for those as was buried in unhallowed ground. Nobody tells *me* what to do or where to go." She glared at the door. "I don't like that man," she said. "I'm going to see what he's doing."

A flicker, and Bod was alone in the room once

more. He heard a rumble of distant thunder.

In the cluttered darkness of Bolger's Antiquities, Abanazer Bolger looked up suspiciously, certain that someone was watching him, then realized he was being foolish. "The boy's locked in the room," he told himself. "The front door's locked." He was polishing the metal clasp surrounding the snakestone, as gently and as carefully as an archaeologist on a dig, taking off the black and revealing the glittering silver beneath it.

He was beginning to regret calling Tom Hustings over, although Hustings was big and good for scaring people. He was also beginning to regret that he was going to have to sell the brooch when he was done. It was special. The more it glittered, under the tiny light on his counter, the more he wanted it to be his, and only his.

There was more where this came from, though. The boy would tell him. The boy would lead him to it.

The boy . . .

And then an idea struck him. He put down the brooch reluctantly, and opened a drawer behind the counter, taking out a metal biscuit tin filled with envelopes and cards and slips of paper.

He reached in, and took out a card only slightly larger than a business card. It was black edged. There was no name or address printed on it, though. Only one word, handwritten in the center in an ink that had faded to brown: *Jack*.

On the back of the card, in pencil, Abanazer Bolger had written instructions to himself, in his tiny, precise handwriting, as a reminder, although he would not have been likely to forget the use of the card, how to use it to summon the man Jack. No, not summon. *Invite*. You did not summon people like him.

A knocking on the outer door of the shop.

Bolger tossed the card down onto the counter, and walked over to the door, peering out into the wet afternoon.

"Hurry up," called Tom Hustings. "It's miserable out here. Dismal. I'm getting soaked."

Bolger unlocked the door and Tom Hustings pushed his way in, his raincoat and hair dripping. "What's so important that you can't talk about it over the phone, then?"

"Our fortune," said Abanazer Bolger, with his sour

face. "That's what."

Hustings took off his raincoat and hung it on the back of the shop door. "What is it? Something good fell off the back of a lorry?"

"Treasure," said Abanazer Bolger. "Two kinds." He took his friend over to the counter, showed him the brooch, under the little light.

"It's old, isn't it?"

"From pagan times," said Abanazer. "Before. From Druid times. Before the Romans came. It's called a snakestone. Seen 'em in museums. I've never seen metalwork like that, or one so fine. Must have belonged to a king. The lad who found it says it come from a grave—think of a barrow filled with stuff like this."

"Might be worth doing it legit," said Hustings thoughtfully. "Declare it as treasure trove. They have to pay us market value for it, and we could make them name it for us. The Hustings-Bolger Bequest."

"Bolger-Hustings," said Abanazer automatically. Then he said, "There's a few people I know of, people with real money, would pay more than market value, if they could hold it as you are—" for Tom

Hustings was fingering the brooch gently, like a man stroking a kitten—"and there'd be no questions asked." He reached out his hand and, reluctantly, Tom Hustings passed him the brooch.

"You said two kinds of treasure," said Hustings. "What's t'other?"

Abanazer Bolger picked up the black-edged card, held it out for his friend's inspection. "Do you know what this is?"

His friend shook his head.

Abanazer put the card down on the counter. "There's a party is looking for another party."

"So?"

"The way I heard it," said Abanazer Bolger, "the other party is a boy."

"There's boys everywhere," said Tom Hustings. "Running all around. Getting into trouble. I can't abide them. So, there's a party looking for a particular boy?"

"This lad looks to be the right sort of age. He's dressed—well, you'll see how he's dressed. And he found this. It could be him."

"And if it is him?"

Abanazer Bolger picked up the card again, by

the edge, and waved it back and forth slowly, as if running the edge along an imaginary flame. "Here comes a candle to light you to bed . . ." he began.

". . . and here comes a chopper to chop off your head," concluded Tom Hustings thoughtfully. "But look you. If you call the man Jack, you lose the boy. And if you lose the boy, you lose the treasure."

And the two men went back and forth on it, weighing the merits and disadvantages of reporting the boy or of collecting the treasure, which had grown in their minds to a huge underground cavern filled with precious things, and as they debated Abanazer pulled a bottle of sloe gin from beneath the counter and poured them both a generous tot, "to assist the cerebrations."

Liza was soon bored with their discussions, which went around and around like a whirligig, getting nowhere, and so she went back into the storeroom, to find Bod standing in the middle of the room with his eyes tightly closed and his fists clenched and his face all screwed up as if he had a toothache, almost purple from holding his breath.

"What you a-doin' of now?" she asked, unimpressed.

He opened his eyes and relaxed. "Trying to Fade," he said.

Liza sniffed. "Try again," she said.

He did, holding his breath even longer this time.

"Stop that," she told him, "or you'll pop."

Bod took a deep breath and then sighed. "It doesn't work," he said. "Maybe I could hit him with a rock and just run for it." There wasn't a rock, so he picked up a colored-glass paperweight, hefted it in his hand, wondering if he could throw it hard enough to stop Abanazer Bolger in his tracks.

"There's two of them out there now," said Liza. "And if the one don't get you, t'other one will. They say they want to get you to show them where you got the brooch, and then dig up the grave and take the treasure." She did not tell him about the other discussions they were having, nor about the black-edged card. She shook her head. "Why did you do something as stupid as this anyway? You know the rules about leaving the graveyard. Just asking for trouble, it was."

Bod felt very insignificant, and very foolish. "I wanted to get you a headstone," he admitted in a small voice. "And I thought it would cost more money. So I was going to sell him the brooch, to buy you your headstone."

She didn't say anything.

"Are you angry?"

She shook her head. "It's the first nice thing anyone's done for me in five hundred years," she said with a hint of a goblin smile. "Why would I be angry?" Then she said, "What do you do, when you try to Fade?"

"What Mr. Pennyworth told me. *'I am an empty doorway, I am a vacant alley, I am nothing. Eyes will not see me, glances slip over me.'* But it never works."

"It's because you're alive," said Liza with a sniff. "There's stuff as works for us, the dead, who have to fight to be noticed at the best of times, that won't never work for you people."

She hugged herself tightly, moving her body back and forth, as if she was debating something. Then she said, "It's because of me you got into this. . . . Come here, Nobody Owens."

He took a step toward her, in that tiny room, and she put her cold hand on his forehead. It felt like a wet silk scarf against his skin.

"Now," she said. "Perhaps I can do a good turn for you."

And with that, she began to mutter to herself, mumbling words that Bod could not make out. Then she said, clear and loud,

"Be hole, be dust, be dream, be wind,
Be night, be dark, be wish, be mind,
Now slip, now slide, now move unseen,
Above, beneath, betwixt, between."

Something huge touched him, brushed him from head to feet, and he shivered. His hair prickled, and his skin was all gooseflesh. Something had changed. "What did you do?" he asked.

"Just gave you a helping hand," she said. "I may be dead, but I'm a dead witch, remember. And we don't forget."

"But—"

"Hush up," she said. "They're coming back."

The key rattled in the storeroom lock. "Now then, chummy," said a voice Bod had not heard clearly before, "I'm sure we're all going to be great friends," and with that Tom Hustings pushed open the door. Then he stood in the doorway looking around, looking puzzled. He was a big, big man, with foxy-red hair and a bottle-red nose. "Here. Abanazer? I thought you said he was in here."

"I did," said Bolger from behind him.

"Well, I can't see hide nor hair of him."

Bolger's face appeared behind the ruddy man's and he peered into the room. "Hiding," he said, staring straight at where Bod was standing. "No use hiding," he announced loudly. "I can see you there. Come on out."

The two men walked into the little room, and Bod stood stock-still between them and thought of Mr. Pennyworth's lessons. He did not react, he did not move. He let the men's glances slide over him without seeing him.

"You're going to wish you'd come out when I called," said Bolger, and he shut the door. "Right," he said to Tom Hustings. "You block the door, so he can't get past." And with that he walked around the room, peering behind things, and bending awkwardly, to look beneath the desk. He walked straight past Bod and opened the cupboard. "Now I see you!" he shouted. "Come out!"

Liza giggled.

"What was that?" asked Tom Hustings, spinning around.

"I didn't hear nothing," said Abanazer Bolger.

Liza giggled again. Then she put her lips together and blew, making a noise that began as a whistling and then sounded like a distant wind. The electric lights in the little room flickered and buzzed. Then they went out.

"Bloody fuses," said Abanazer Bolger. "Come on. This is a waste of time."

The key clicked in the lock, and Liza and Bod were left alone in the room.

"He's got away," said Abanazer Bolger. Bod could hear him now, through the door. "Room like that. There wasn't anywhere he could have been hiding. We'd've seen him if he was."

"The man Jack won't like that."

"Who's going to tell him?"

A pause.

"Here. Tom Hustings. Where's the brooch gone?"

"Mm? That? Here. I was keeping it safe."

"Keeping it safe? In your pocket? Funny place to be keeping it safe, if you ask me. More like you were planning to make off with it—like you was planning to keep my brooch for your own."

"Your brooch, Abanazer? *Your* brooch? Our

brooch, you mean."

"Ours, indeed. I don't remember you being here when I got it from that boy."

"That boy that you couldn't even keep safe for the man Jack, you mean? Can you imagine what he'll do, when he finds *you* had the boy he was looking for, and *you* let him go?"

"Probably not the same boy. Lots of boys in the world—what're the odds it was the one he was looking for? Out the back door as soon as my back was turned, I'll bet." And then Abanazer Bolger said, in a high, wheedling voice, "Don't you worry about the man Jack, Tom Hustings. I'm sure that it was a different boy. My old mind playing tricks. And we're almost out of sloe gin—how would you fancy a good Scotch? I've whiskey in the back room. You just wait here a moment."

The storeroom door was unlocked, and Abanazer entered, holding a walking stick and a flashlight, looking even more sour of face than before.

"If you're still in here," he said in a sour mutter, "don't even think of making a run for it. I've called the police on you, that's what I've done." A rummage in a drawer produced the half-filled bottle of whiskey, and then a tiny black bottle. Abanazer poured several drops from the little bottle into the larger, then he pocketed the tiny bottle. "My brooch, and mine alone," he mouthed, and followed it with a barked, "Just coming, Tom!"

He glared around the dark room, staring past Bod, then he left the storeroom, carrying the whiskey in front of him. He locked the door behind him.

"Here you go," came Abanazer Bolger's voice through the door. "Give us your glass then, Tom. Nice drop of Scotch, put hairs on your chest. Say when."

Silence. "Cheap muck. Aren't you drinking?"

"That sloe gin's gone to my innards. Give it a minute for my stomach to settle. . . ." Then, "Here—Tom! What have you done with my brooch?"

"*Your* brooch is it now? Whoa—I feel a bit queasy . . . you put something in my drink, you little grub!"

"What if I did? I could read on your face what you was planning, Tom Hustings. Thief."

And then there was shouting, and several crashes, and loud bangs, as if heavy items of furniture were being overturned . . .

. . . then silence.

Liza said, "Quickly now. Let's get you out of here."

"But the door's locked." He looked at her. "Is there something you can do to get us out?"

"Me? I don't have any magics will get you out of a locked room, boy."

Bod crouched, and peered out through the keyhole. It was blocked; the key sat in the keyhole. Bod thought, then he smiled momentarily, and it lit his face like the flash of a lightbulb. He pulled a crumpled sheet of newspaper from a packing case, flattened it out as best he could, then pushed it underneath the door, leaving only a corner on his side of the doorway.

"What are you playing at?" asked Liza impatiently.

"I need something like a pencil. Only thinner . . ." he said. "Here we go." And he took a thin paintbrush from the top of the desk, and pushed the brushless end into the lock, jiggled it, and pushed some more.

There was a muffled *clunk* as the key was pushed out, as it dropped from the lock onto the newspaper. Bod pulled the paper back under the door, now with the key sitting on it.

Liza laughed, delighted. "That's wit, young man,"

she said. "That's wisdom."

Bod put the key in the lock, turned it, and pushed open the storeroom door.

There were two men on the floor in the middle of the crowded antique shop. Furniture had indeed fallen; the place was a chaos of wrecked clocks and chairs, and in the midst of it the bulk of Tom Hustings lay, fallen on the smaller figure of Abanazer Bolger. Neither of them was moving.

"Are they dead?" asked Bod.

"No such luck," said Liza.

On the floor beside the men was a brooch of glittering silver; a crimson-orange-banded stone, held in place with claws and with snake heads, and the expression on the snake heads was one of triumph and avarice and satisfaction.

Bod dropped the brooch into his pocket, where it sat beside the heavy glass paperweight, the paintbrush, and the little pot of paint.

"Take this too," said Liza.

Bod looked at the black-edged card with the word *Jack* handwritten on one side. It disturbed him. There was something familiar about it, something that stirred old memories, something dangerous. "I don't want it."

"You can't leave it here with them," said Liza. "They were going to use it to hurt you."

"I don't want it," said Bod. "It's bad. Burn it."

"No!" Liza gasped. "Don't do that. You mustn't do that."

"Then I'll give it to Silas," said Bod. And he put the little card into an envelope, so he had to touch it as little as possible, and put the envelope into the inside pocket of his old gardening jacket beside his heart.

Two hundred miles away, the man Jack woke from his sleep, and sniffed the air. He walked downstairs.

"What is it?" asked his grandmother, stirring the contents of a big iron pot on the stove. "What's got into you now?"

"I don't know," he said. "Something's happening. Something . . . interesting." And then he licked his lips. "Smells tasty," he said. "Very tasty."

Lightning illuminated the cobbled street.

Bod hurried through the rain through the Old Town, always heading up the hill toward the graveyard. The gray day had become an early night while he was inside the storeroom, and it came as no surprise to him when a familiar shadow swirled beneath the streetlamps. Bod hesitated, and a flutter of night-black velvet resolved itself into man-shape.

Silas stood in front of him, arms folded. He strode forward impatiently.

"Well?" he said.

Bod said, "I'm sorry, Silas."

"I'm disappointed in you, Bod," Silas said, and he shook his head. "I've been looking for you since I woke. You have the smell of trouble all around you. And you know you're not allowed to go out here, into the living world."

"I know. I'm sorry." There was rain on the boy's face, running down like tears.

"First of all, we need to get you back to safety." Silas reached down and enfolded the living child inside his cloak, and Bod felt the ground fall away beneath him.

"Silas," he said.

Silas did not answer.

"I *was* a bit scared," he said. "But I knew you'd

come and get me if it got too bad. And Liza was there. She helped a lot."

"Liza?" Silas's voice was sharp.

"The witch. From the potter's field."

"And you say she helped you?"

"Yes. She especially helped me with my Fading. I think I can do it now."

Silas grunted. "You can tell me all about it when we're home." And Bod was quiet until they landed beside the church. They went inside, into the empty hall, as the rain redoubled, splashing up from the puddles that covered the ground.

Bod produced the envelope containing the black-edged card. "Um," he said. "I thought you should have this. Well, Liza did, really."

Silas looked at it. Then he opened it, removed the card, stared at it, turned it over, and read Abanazer Bolger's penciled note to himself, in tiny handwriting, explaining the precise manner of use of the card.

"Tell me everything," he said.

Bod told him everything he could remember about the day. And at the end, Silas shook his head slowly, thoughtfully.

"Am I in trouble?" asked Bod.

"Nobody Owens," said Silas. "You are indeed in trouble. However, I believe I shall leave it to your foster parents to administer whatever discipline and reproach they believe to be needed. In the meantime, I need to deal with this."

The black-edged card vanished inside the velvet cloak, and then, in the manner of his kind, Silas was gone.

Bod pulled the jacket up over his head, and clambered up the slippery paths to the top of the hill, to the Frobisher vault, and then he went down, and down, and still farther down.

He dropped the brooch beside the goblet and the knife.

"Here you go," he said. "All polished up. Looking pretty."

IT COMES BACK, whispered the Sleer, with satisfaction in its smoke-tendril voice. IT ALWAYS COMES BACK.

The night had been long, but it was almost dawn.

Bod was walking, sleepily and a little gingerly, past the small tomb of the wonderfully named Miss Liberty Roach (*What she spent is lost, what she gave*

away remains with her always. Reader, be charitable),
past the final resting place of Harrison Westwood,
Baker of this Parish, and his wives, Marion and Joan,
to the potter's field. Mr. and Mrs. Owens had died
several hundred years before it had been decided
that beating children was wrong, and Mr. Owens
had, regretfully, that night, done what he saw as his
duty, and Bod's bottom stung like anything. Still, the
look of worry on Mrs. Owens's face had hurt Bod
worse than any beating could have done.

He reached the iron railings that bounded the
potter's field, and slipped between them.

"Hullo?" he called. There was no answer. Not even
an extra shadow in the hawthorn bush. "I hope I
didn't get you into trouble too," he said.

Nothing.

He had replaced the jeans in the gardener's hut—
he was more comfortable in just his gray winding
sheet—but he had kept the jacket. He liked having
the pockets.

When he had gone to the shed to return the jeans,
he had taken a small hand scythe from the wall
where it hung, and with it he had attacked the nettle
patch in the potter's field, sending the nettles flying,

slashing and gutting them till there was nothing but stinging stubble on the ground.

From his pocket he took the large glass paperweight, its insides a multitude of bright colors, along with the paintpot, and the paintbrush.

He dipped the brush into the paint and carefully painted, in brown paint, on the surface of the paperweight, the letters

E H

and beneath them he wrote

We don't forget

It was almost daylight. Bedtime, soon, and it would not be wise for him to be late to bed for some time to come.

He put the paperweight down on the ground that had once been a nettle patch, placed it in the place that he estimated her head would have been, and, pausing only to look at his handiwork for a moment, he went through the railings and made his way, rather less gingerly, back up the hill.

"Not bad," said a pert voice from the potter's field behind him. "Not bad at all."

But when he turned to look, there was nobody there.

Instructions

Touch the wooden gate in the wall you never saw
  before,
Say "please" before you open the latch,
go through,
walk down the path.
A red metal imp hangs from the
  green-painted front door,
as a knocker,
do not touch it; it will bite your fingers.
Walk through the house. Take nothing. Eat nothing.
However,
if any creature tells you that it hungers,
feed it.
If it tells you that it is dirty,
clean it.
If it cries to you that it hurts,
if you can,
ease its pain.

From the back garden you will be able to see the wild
   wood.
The deep well you walk past leads down to Winter's
   realm;
there is another land at the bottom of it.
If you turn around here,
you can walk back, safely;
you will lose no face. I will think no less of you.

Once through the garden you will be in the wood.
The trees are old. Eyes peer from the undergrowth.
Beneath a twisted oak sits an old woman.
   She may ask for something;
give it to her. She
will point the way to the castle. Inside it
are three princesses.
Do not trust the youngest. Walk on.
In the clearing beyond the castle the
   twelve months sit about a fire,
warming their feet, exchanging tales.
They may do favors for you, if you are polite.
You may pick strawberries in December's frost.

Trust the wolves, but do not tell them
      where you are going.
The river can be crossed by the ferry.
      The ferryman will take you.
(The answer to his question is this:
If he hands the oar to his passenger, he
      will be free to leave the boat.
Only tell him this from a safe distance.)

If an eagle gives you a feather, keep it safe.
Remember: that giants sleep too soundly; that
witches are often betrayed by their appetites;
dragons have one soft spot, somewhere, always;
hearts can be well hidden,
and you betray them with your tongue.
Do not be jealous of your sister:
know that diamonds and roses
are as uncomfortable when they tumble
      from one's lips as toads and frogs:
colder, too, and sharper, and they cut.

Remember your name.
Do not lose hope—what you seek will be found.
Trust ghosts. Trust those that you have

helped to help you in their turn.
Trust dreams.
Trust your heart, and trust your story.

When you come back, return the way you came.
Favors will be returned, debts be repaid.
Do not forget your manners.
Do not look back.
Ride the wise eagle (you shall not fall)
Ride the silver fish (you will not drown)
Ride the gray wolf (hold tightly to his fur).

There is a worm at the heart of the tower;
      that is why it will not stand.

When you reach the little house, the
      place your journey started,
you will recognize it, although it will seem
      much smaller than you remember.
Walk up the path, and through the garden
      gate you never saw before but once.
And then go home. Or make a home.

Or rest.